Hiccup and pet dragon Toothless

ABOUT THE AUTHOR

Hiccup Horrendous Haddock the Third was
an awesome swordfighter, a dragon-whisperer,
and the greatest Viking Hero that ever lived.
But Hiccup's memoirs look back to when he was
a very ordinary boy, and finding it hard to be a
Hero. In this third volume, Hiccup is captured by
the Romans and pays his first terrifying visit
to the gladitorial arena...

More books about Hiccup:

How to Train Your Dragon
How to be a Pirate
How to Cheat a Dragon's Curse
How to Twist a Dragon's Tale

I dedicate this book to Maisie and Clementine

**A big thank you to Simon Cowell, Caspar Hare and
Andrea Malaskova**

Text and illustrations copyright © 2005 Cressida Cowell

First published in Great Britain in 2005 by Hodder Children's Books

The right of Cressida Cowell to be identified as the
Author of this Work has been asserted by her in accordance
with the Copyright, Designs and Patents Act 1988.

13

A Catalogue record for this book is available from the British Library

ISBN-13: 978 0 340 89304 3

Text design by Cressida Cowell and Nigel Baines
Printed and bound in Great Britain by CPI Bookmarque, Croydon

The paper and board used in this paperback by Hodder Children's Books are natural
recyclable products made from wood grown in sustainable forests. The manufacturing
processes conform to the environmental regulations of the country of origin.

Hodder Children's Books
a division of Hachette Children's Books
338 Euston Road, London NW1 3BH
An Hachette Livre UK Company

Please note....
The Dark Ages were so very, very dark
it is sometimes difficult to separate
FACT from FICTION.

How to Speak Dragonese

by
Hiccup Horrendous Haddock III

translated from the Old Norse by
CRESSIDA COWELL

Hodder Children's Books

A division of Hachette Children's Books

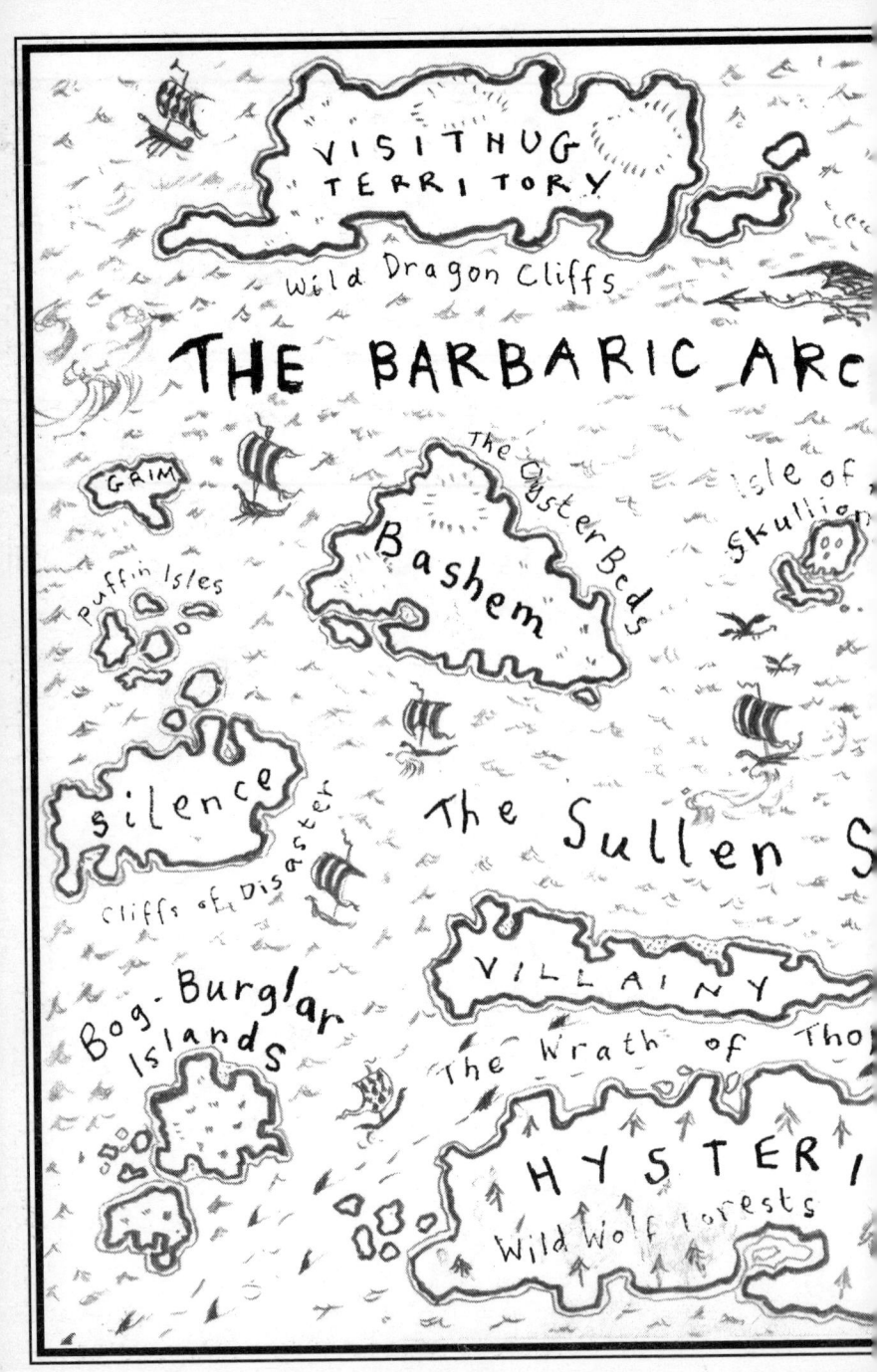

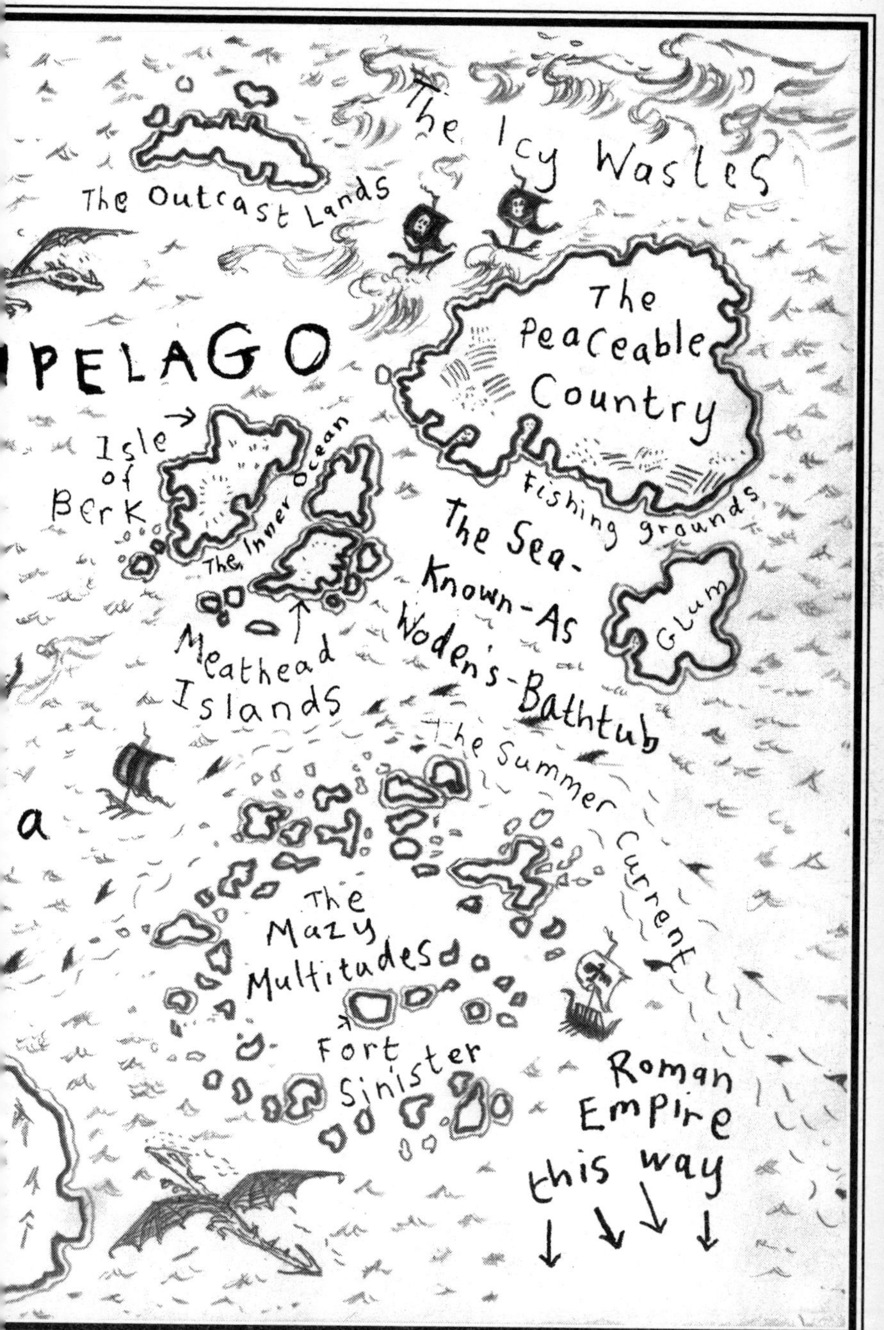

The Icy Wastes

The Outcast Lands

The Peaceable Country

...PELAGO

Isle of Berk

The Inner Ocean

fishing grounds

Meathead Islands

The Sea-Known-As Woden's-Bathtub

Glum

The Summer Current

a

The Mazy Multitudes

Fort Sinister

Roman Empire this way
↓ ↓ ↓ ↓

~ CONTENTS ~

Hiccup and his
sword, Endeavour

Once there were dragons.

Imagine a time of **DRAGONS** – some larger than mountainsides, slumbering in the depths of the ocean; some smaller than your fingernail, hopping through the heather.

Imagine a time of **VIKING HEROES**, in which men were men and women were sort of men too and even some little babies had chest hair.

And now imagine that you are a boy called Hiccup Horrendous Haddock the Third, not yet twelve years old and not yet turning out to be the kind of Hero his father would have liked him to be. That boy of course, was really ME, but the boy I was then seems so far away to me now that I shall tell this story almost as if he were a stranger.

So, imagine that instead of being me, this stranger, this Hero-in-Waiting, is **YOU**.

You are small. You have red hair. You don't realise it yet, but you are about to set out on the most alarming episode of your life so far… When you are an old, old man like I am you will call it 'My First Encounter with the Roman Empire' – and even at this distance in time it will still cause your old wrinkled arms to prickle with goose bumps as you remember the perils and dangers of that terrifying adventure…

1. THE BOARDING-AN-ENEMY-SHIP LESSON

Once upon a foggy day in a cold, cold country long, long ago, seven small Viking boats floated through the Sea-Known-as-Woden's-Bathtub. The fog had swallowed up the Peaceable Country to the north, and the Isle of Berk to the west, and, indeed, had swallowed up so much of everything, that it was as if the boats were sky-boats, and had left the earth entirely, and were sailing through cloud banks way, way up in the air.

In the first boat, *The Fat Boar*, sat Gobber the Belch, a six and a half foot giant in teeny-weeny hairy shorts, who had leg muscles so enormous they had muscles of their own, and a beard like a hedgehog struck by lightning. Gobber was the teacher in charge of the Pirate Training Programme on the Isle of Berk, and this sail through the fog was part of a Boarding-an-Enemy-Ship lesson.

The six boy-sized boats that were following *The Fat Boar* each had two boys in them, and these boys were Gobber's pupils, young members of the Tribe of the Hairy Hooligans.

'OK, YOU DISGUSTING GLOBS OF GIRLY SNOT!' yelled Gobber, in a bellow so loud it could be heard several miles away. 'WE ARE NOW GOING TO PRACTISE BOARDING AN ENEMY SHIP ON THE EASY TARGET OF A PEACEABLE FISHING BOAT... CAN ANYONE REMEMBER THE FIRST RULE OF AMBUSH?'

'TAKE THE ENEMY BY SURPRISE, SIR!' shouted out Snotface Snotlout, a tall, unpleasantly smug-looking boy with gigantic nostrils and the beginnings of a small moustache.

'Very good, Snotlout,' purred Gobber the Belch, and he continued at full volume: 'IN A FOG THIS THICK YOUR VICTIM SHIP WILL NOT HAVE A CHANCE OF SEEING YOU COMING!'

They can hear *us, though*, thought Hiccup Horrendous Haddock the Third, gloomily trying to peer through the fog, *unless, of course, we have the luck to stumble across some completely* deaf *Peaceable fishermen...*

Hiccup Horrendous Haddock the Third is, rather surprisingly, the Hero of this story. I say surprisingly, because the first thing you noticed about Hiccup was how very, very ordinary he was. He was on the small side, with a slightly freckled, absolutely average face that would always get overlooked in a crowd.

His dragon, Toothless, who was at that moment asleep down the front of Hiccup's shirt, was just as average as his owner. The only truly remarkable thing about Toothless was how remarkably *small* he was. He was at least half the size of the other boys' dragons.

And, as you can imagine, this wasn't something to boast about.

Gobber's shouting woke the little dragon up. He poked his nose out of the neck of Hiccup's tunic. 'W-w-what's happening?' he asked sleepily in Dragonese.*

---

* Dragons spoke Dragonese. Only Hiccup could understand this fascinating language.

'Oh, nothing unusual,' Hiccup whispered back, scratching Toothless behind the horns. (He loved that.) 'Gobber is shouting, Snotlout is showing off, and we're all out here floating in the fog and the cold when we could be tucked up in front of a roasting fire... you can go back to sleep if you like.'

Toothless chuckled. 'You V-v-vikings are as m-m-mad as mackerel,' he said. 'W-w-wake Toothless up when it's l-l-lunchtime...' And he burrowed back down to the nice warm spot just next to Hiccup's left armpit and closed his eyes again.

Hiccup was sharing his boat with his best friend Fishlegs, who was even skinnier than Hiccup and looked a lot like a daddy-long-legs with asthma and a squint. Fishlegs put his hand up in the air.

'It's all very well that they can't see us coming, sir,' he pointed out logically, 'but how are *we* going to see them so we can board *them* in the first place?'

'Easy-peasy, o plankton-brain,' boomed Gobber, very pleased with himself. 'Peaceable fishing boats are always followed by flocks of Lesser

Blackbacked Seadragons, hoping for a bite. All you have to do is follow the racket they make and you'll have found yourself a boat. You then simply board the boat yelling the Hooligan War Cry: repeat after me... YAAAAAAAAAH!' yelled Gobber the Belch.

'YAAAAAAAAAH!' yelled ten of the boys back at him, brandishing their swords like maniacs.

'Yaaaaah,' repeated Hiccup and Fishlegs, without much enthusiasm.

'The Peaceables are terrified of us Hooligans, Woden only knows why… Right, lads – you steal one of their helmets to prove you have completed the exercise, and report back to me. THIS IS GOING TO BE LIKE BURGLING BERRIES FROM A BABY!' boomed Gobber the Belch.

'Oh, I nearly forgot. Silly me… ' Gobber laughed carelessly. 'The one thing you *do* have to bear in mind is that ON NO ACCOUNT SHOULD YOU LEAVE THIS BAY. This is VERY IMPORTANT because just to the south of here runs the Summer Current, a warm stream of water, and you all know what lives in the Summer Current…'

'Sharkworms,' gulped Fishlegs.

'That's right, Fishlegs,' boomed Gobber. 'I know Hiccup, our natural history expert, can tell us something about Sharkworms.'

'Certainly sir,' replied Hiccup, delighted to be asked a question about his favourite subject, dragons. He took out of his pocket a small scruffy notebook with *How to Speak Dragonese* written in large scrawly letters on the front. In this book Hiccup kept notes on the Dragonese language and descriptions of the various species of dragons and their habits.

'Well,' said Hiccup, having trouble reading his own handwriting, 'Sharkworms are a kind of dragon that look a lot like sharks. The adults can grow to about six metres in length, they have at least five rows of teeth—'

'GET ON WITH IT, BOY!' yelled Gobber.

'They are highly carnivorous and they not only scavenge off ships but climb aboard and attack you there... On land they can easily outrun a man... I would suggest, sir, that if there was even a *chance* we could run into Sharkworms we should leave the area immediately.'

'For Thor's sake, boy,' grinned Gobber the Belch, 'with that kind of attitude you might never leave the house. I'm training you to be *pirates*, not *softies*.'

'What happens if we get lost, sir?' pleaded Fishlegs.

'Lost?' snorted Gobber. 'LOST! Vikings don't get LOST!'

'Honestly, sir,' sneered Snotface Snotlout, 'I don't know why you don't throw Hiccup the Useless and his fishlegged failure of a friend out of the Tribe completely. They're a disgrace to all of us.'

Hiccup and Fishlegs looked miserable.

'I mean look at their *boat*, sir,' continued the sneering Snotlout. 'We're *Vikings*, sir, the greatest shipbuilders the Ancient World has ever known, sir. A raft like that just makes us look ridiculous.'

'You think you're so clever, Snotlout,' retorted Hiccup determinedly, 'but this boat can go a lot faster than you think. Looks aren't everything, you know...'

Unfortunately, Snotlout had a point.

The Hopeful Puffin was more of a floating accident than an actual boat.

She had been built by Hiccup and Fishlegs in Shipbuilding lessons, and they were both hopeless at woodwork. Something kept on going wrong with the design and instead of being long and thin like a Viking ship should be, she had ended up fat and almost completely round. Her mast was too long and leaned lopsidedly to the left, so that in a strong wind she went round in circles.

She also had a leak.

Every half an hour Fishlegs or Hiccup had to remember to bail out the seawater that had collected in the bottom of the boat with Hiccup's helmet (Fishlegs's helmet also had a leak).

Gobber the Belch looked at *The Hopeful Puffin*.

'Mmm,' said Gobber thoughtfully. 'You might have a point, Snotlout. NOW!' he continued briskly.

'At the sound of my horn, the exercise will begin.'

He raised a curly-wurly bugle to his lips.

'Ooooh, jumping jellyfish,' moaned Fishlegs, 'I HATE the Pirate Training Programme! We're going to get lost… we're going to sink… we're going to get eaten slowly by Sharkworms…'

'S-C-R-E-E-E-ECH!' screamed the bugle.

The Hopeful Puffin

23

2. SHARKWORMS

Just as the sound of the bugle died away, the fog lifted, for a second giving a glimpse of the entire bay. Over to the right, further towards the grey outline of the Peaceable Country, there were the shadowy shapes of four or five Peaceable fishing boats, surrounded by clouds of screeching Blackbacked Seadragons.

'Over there!' yelled Sharpknife and Tuffnut Junior, turning their boat, *The Raven*.

'It's all under control, Fishlegs!' shouted Hiccup excitedly. 'I can see where we're going!' Hiccup yanked the rudder of *The Hopeful Puffin* so sharply that Fishlegs lost his balance and fell face first into the water at the bottom of the boat.

The wind caught the sails at exactly the right speed and *The Hopeful Puffin* surged forward after the others... But Hiccup hadn't noticed Snotlout's boat, *Sparrowhawk*, steaming up behind him at great speed.

Sparrowhawk was as lean and mean and hungry as Snotlout himself. Beautifully built out of elm wood, she came to a point so sharp at the prow that she sliced through the water as easily as an axe through a

scallop. She was being steered by Dogsbreath the Duhbrain, Snotlout's best friend – a great, hairy bully of a boy with a ring through his nose, who was snorting so hard with laughter that snot flew in all directions.

'Get him, Fireworm,' whispered Snotface Snotlout, and his dragon, a glistening blood-red Monstrous Nightmare, leaped from Snotlout's shoulder and dive-bombed Hiccup from behind with a furious shriek.

Fireworm swooped down and pushed Hiccup's helmet down over his eyes with her talons. Hiccup took his hands off the rudder in surprise, and at the same moment, *Sparrowhawk* rammed into the port

Snotlout's friend DOGSBREATH

side of *The Hopeful Puffin*, denting her severely.

'So sorry, Useless!' jeered Snotface Snotlout, as *Sparrowhawk* sailed on, completely unhurt. 'Your pathetic raft is so small we didn't see you!'

'Har har har,' guffawed Dogsbreath the Duhbrain.

The ramming sent *The Hopeful Puffin* into one of her spins.

For a long time she spun round in wobbly circles, like a confused

Sparrowhawk

sea-urchin.
Eventually, Hiccup
regained control of the
rudder and Fishlegs picked
himself up from the bottom of the boat,
moaning slightly.

The Hopeful Puffin completed her final spin
and began moving swiftly forwards.

But the fog had come down again, if anything
even thicker than before. After all that spinning,

Hiccup had absolutely no idea which direction they were facing. And when the last faint echoes of Snotlout and Dogsbreath's jeering had faded away, they sailed on in spooky silence.

'Where is everybody?' asked Fishlegs.

'Ssssh,' scolded Hiccup. 'I'm trying to listen.'

The boys were quiet for ten long minutes.

The only sound to be heard was the lapping of water against the sides of the boat and a brisk wind filling out the sail. They were gliding along at quite a rate now, but where were they going? Hiccup and Fishlegs strained their eyes into the fog and their ears into the silence, desperate to see or hear something, anything at all.

But there was nothing.

It might have been Hiccup's imagination playing tricks on him, but it seemed to him as if the air suddenly felt just a *tiny* bit warmer, and when he trailed a finger briefly into the water it felt just a *tiny* bit less icy than it should have done. And then he got to thinking about the Summer Current and Sharkworms and a prickle of fear ran all down his back, and everywhere about him the drifting, ghostly fog seemed to be taking the shape of Sharkworm fins…

'Just out of interest,' asked Fishlegs casually, 'how does a Sharkworm attack you, exactly?'

'Well,' replied Hiccup, changing direction yet again in the hope of getting back to the safety of the bay, 'Sharkworms *should* only attack if you are wounded. Even if you're not in the water they can smell the blood and that drives them crazy. And then, because they have legs as well as a fishy tail, they can actually CLIMB ABOARD a ship to get you. That's where they got their nickname of "Pirate Dragons", because, although they can survive at least ten minutes in the air, they generally drag you back into the water to kill you.'

'Oh, *brilliant*,' said Fishlegs, frantically checking himself all over to see if he had any grazes. 'Do you think eczema counts or does it have to be an actual *cut*?'

'I'm not sure,' said Hiccup. 'I've never actually met a Sharkworm.'

'Better and better,' said Fishlegs. 'It's at times like this that I am *so glad* that I was born a Viking and not a Roman.' (The Romans were the Vikings' deadly enemies – a very bossy lot who wanted to take over the world and had jolly nearly got there.) 'Think how BORING it would be to be a Roman. All those warm baths and lounging around in togas when you could be out here enjoying the fresh air and the multi-fanged blood-crazy carnivores…'

'Ssssh,' said Hiccup, changing direction for the ninth time. 'Let's just see whether we can hear anything this time…'

But again there was silence, and the splash of seawater coming over the side on to Hiccup's ankle felt definitely warm.

'I'm h-h-hungry,' said a deep little voice from Hiccup's chest and both boys jumped at the sudden sound.

The nose of Toothless, Hiccup's disobedient little dragon, poked out of the top of Hiccup's shirt, closely followed by the rest of him. He crawled sleepily up Hiccup's neck to his familiar perch on the top of Hiccup's helmet, where he shook out his wings, had a quick rummage for dragonfleas, and gave an enormous yawn, revealing a very pink forked tongue and the fang-free gums that gave him his name.

Even though he was only a Common-or-Garden dragon, the most ordinary of the dragon species, Toothless was a beautiful little creature. He was a deep emerald green in colour, fading to shimmering pearl on his tummy like a mackerel, lightly sprinkled with pale brown freckles. Enormous, innocent, grass-green eyes peered out from between absurdly long eyelashes.

Appearances, of course, were deceptive, for dragons are among the most selfish animals on the planet, and Toothless was, in fact, a shark in a baby seal's clothing.

'You can help us, actually, Toothless,' said Hiccup. 'This is IMPORTANT. We need to find ourselves back to the bay. We're a bit worried that we might have accidentally got ourselves into the Summer Current and we don't want to bump into any SHARKWORMS, now, do we?' Hiccup laughed nervously. 'So what YOU could do is flap around and look for boats so we can get back on the right course.'

'Ask Horrorcow. Toothless h-h-hungry,' said Toothless grumpily. He had woken up in a bad mood.

Hiccup raised his eyes to the heavens before explaining patiently that Horrowcow was asleep and there was no way she was going to wake up.

Horrorcow was Fishlegs's dragon – a nice enough beast, but she spent most of her time asleep. She was lying, sprawled full length, underneath one of the rowing benches. Fishlegs had put a coat under her head to lift it clear of the water so she didn't drown.

'T-t-toothless not m-m-moving.' Toothless was in a big sulk now. 'N-n-no food – no moving. Toothless on strike. Hiccup BOSSY BOSSY BOSSY. D-à-à-do this. Do that. Toothless a à-à-dragon, not a slave. Work, work, work, that's all you make poor Toothless do.'

'Toothless, you've been asleep since breakfast!' protested Hiccup. 'And that's the most unfair thing I've ever heard. I wait on you hand and foot, you know I do. I feed you constantly, I tell you jokes, I carry you everywhere...'

'Toothless h-h-has w-w-weak wings,' said Toothless pathetically.

'You woke me up FOUR TIMES last night...'

'Toothless had a n-n-nightmare.' Toothless opened his big green eyes even wider. 'Great big fat horrible h-h-humans with BIG TEETH chasing poor Toothless all through his b-b-bed, want to get Toothless because Toothless is so s-s-special...'

'You wanted OYSTERS!' howled Hiccup.

'Oysters at three o'clock in the morning!'

'Oysters g-g-good for nightmares,' protested Toothless.

Hiccup ran out of patience.

'You wouldn't shut up! You perched on my father's bed and said you'd screech in his ear if I didn't get them! I had to get up, get dressed, go down to the Oyster Hoard in Hooligan Harbour and then when I got back again you wouldn't even EAT them because you said they were the wrong colour or something!'

'They had b-b-black bits on them,' whined

Toothless. 'Toothless h-h-hates black bits, they're YUCKY...'

'Oh, don't be such a BIG BABY, Toothless,' snapped Hiccup. 'It was only bits of seaweed and even when I picked them all off you STILL wouldn't eat them!'

'I hate to interrupt,' said Fishlegs nervously, 'but I'm pretty certain I saw the fin of a Sharkworm over there...'

But Toothless and Hiccup were so cross they didn't even hear. They were nose to nose, eyeballing each other. Toothless had puffed up to nearly twice his normal size and had turned an unpleasant mustardy-red colour. Hiccup had forgotten you shouldn't really look a dragon in the eye for too long because their gaze is hypnotic, and he was starting to feel dizzy. But he was so angry he didn't care.

This dragon had gone too far this time.

Hiccup had HAD ENOUGH.

He was going to put his foot down.

'I do ALL these things for YOU,' continued Hiccup, 'and EVERY now and then I ask you to do a few SIMPLE things for ME, like catch some mackerel in a Dragontraining Lesson, or look out for

dragon on strike

Sharkworms so we don't all get dragged off and torn to pieces, and what do you do? You go ON STRIKE. Well you've gone too far this time. I've HAD ENOUGH. I'm putting my foot down. You can just GO on strike then and see if I care.'

'OK then,' hissed Toothless. 'T-T-Toothless really WILL go on strike.'

With great dignity Toothless flapped off Hiccup's shoulder and up to the top of the mast where he perched, muttering to himself in a furious undertone, 'T-T-Toothless a BIG BABY, is he? HA! We'll SEE about that, M-M-Mister Smartypants Hiccup. L-l-let's just find out how l-l-long you last without the help of the BIG BABY…'

'What's he doing?' asked Fishlegs.

Fishlegs didn't speak Dragonese, so he wasn't sure what was going on. 'Is he listening out for boats so we can get back to the bay?'

'Er, no…' admitted Hiccup, whose head was still spinning after the staring contest with Toothless. 'We had a bit of a row and he's gone on strike. But I've had it up to here with that dragon. He's pushed me too far too often… I'm drawing a line in the mud…'

'Oh, for Thor's sake!' Fishlegs exploded. 'We haven't got time for that now… LOOK!'

Hiccup's eyes finally swam back into focus.

He looked.

The fog had shifted around, making it difficult to see, but for a moment Hiccup thought he might have glimpsed a black fin, with the jagged edge that made it clear that this was the fin of a Sharkworm, rather than that of its less dangerous relative, the ordinary shark…

'I don't think that *was* a Sharkworm, you know, Fishlegs,' said Hiccup uncertainly. 'I think it's just the fog playing tricks on our eyes…'

But Fishlegs wasn't taking any chances. He

tried to shake Horrorcow awake but the little reptile only snored all the harder.

'We need Toothless!' panicked Fishlegs. 'For Thor's sake *do* something! Apologise! Promise him something large that he can EAT!'

'You could be right,' admitted Hiccup. 'OK, Toothless,' he called up. Through the fog he could just see the dragon-on-strike perched on top of the swaying mast. 'I apologise. We need you. If you fly down and help I'll give you all my supper for the next three weeks!'

'S-s-sixty seconds,' said Toothless to himself with satisfaction. 'Sixty seconds and they n-n-need Toothless again.'

'N-n-not listening!' he sang down, examining his talons. 'H-H-Hiccup not need the help of a BIG BABY...'

'Honestly, I think we're sort of OK,' said Hiccup, squinting at the seas around them. 'I can't see anything now and Sharkworms really are only supposed to attack if somebody has an open wound...'

Fishlegs was too panicked to hear what Hiccup was saying. He started yelling up the mast.

'Toooooothlessssss!'

'Not listening! Not l-l-listening!' Toothless called back with his wings over his ears.

Fishlegs shut his eyes in the hope that this wasn't really happening... and then he opened them again.

'*Listen!*' he hissed with frantic relief. 'Can you hear what I hear? *Sea-dragons!*'

Hiccup sat very still.

And there it was, a very faint noise of dragons shrieking.

'A Peaceable fishing boat!' said Fishlegs joyfully. 'Just in time, too! This is our lucky day!' He grabbed the rudder off Hiccup and swung it hard around to face in the direction of the noise.

'Come on, come ON,' Fishlegs urged *The Hopeful Puffin* as the wind caught her sails and took her swiftly forwards, 'and *please* don't start turning round in circles.'

To Fishlegs's relief the noise of screaming dragons grew louder and louder and the grey shadowy shape of an enormous boat loomed at them out of the fog.

It was a far, far larger boat than Hiccup was expecting. Surely Peaceable fishing boats didn't normally have three layers of oars? And the sound the dragons were making was also unusual.

'Those dragons aren't hungry, they're *angry*,' said Hiccup slowly.

'Who cares?' shrieked Fishlegs, grabbing a grappling hook that was on a rope attached to the prow of *The Hopeful Puffin*. He threw it so that it caught perfectly over the rim of the larger boat and held.

Fishlegs was not a great athlete. He had tried this countless times in Boarding-an-Enemy-Ship Lessons and had never managed to throw it successfully before.

In fact, several times he had nearly knocked himself out in the process. Which just goes to show, it's amazing what a person can do when he feels he is in deadly mortal danger.

'Hang on a second, Fishlegs!' warned Hiccup. 'We have to keep our heads here! We haven't definitely *seen* a Sharkworm yet, have we? And those dragons are screaming the most awful things in Dragonese…'

But Fishlegs was in too much of a twitter of terror to listen to Hiccup.

'Have you forgotten? We're supposed to be boarding a Peaceable fishing boat right now!' he

The SHARKWORM

One of the scariest predators in the ocean. You are not safe either in the water or out, for the Sharkworm has thick muscly alligator legs that allow it to climb on board ship to kill.

~STATISTICS~

COLOURS: Black, green, grey.
ARMED WITH: Serrated Fangs, claws etc... 9
RADAR: Absolutely...... 8
POISON: None...... 0
HUNTING ABILITY: Unbelievable on sea and land... 10
SPEED: Astonishingly quick..... 10
FEAR AND FIGHT FACTOR: Don't get in the water.... 10

Wings fold into body cavity when swimming

scolded. 'Remember Boarding-an-Enemy-Ship lessons? Remember Gobber? Big chap, bad breath, muscles like Bashyballs? He's going to KILL us if we don't come back with a Peaceable helmet, right? Although, of course, it's a fascinating question whether or not that was a deadly man-eating Sharkworm or just a trick of the eyes, I really don't feel like staying here and discussing it somehow...'

Fishlegs started climbing the rope.

Again, Fishlegs was normally hopeless at rope-climbing. But this time he was up that rope as quick as a Shortwing Squirrelserpent scrambling up a tree.

Hiccup hopped nervously from one foot to another, listening to the furiously angry dragons shrieking from the enormous ship towering above him.

He couldn't let Fishlegs board the ship alone.

Hiccup said a quick prayer to Woden, put his hands upon the rope, and began to squirm up after his friend.

'Here goes...' muttered Fishlegs, as he reached the top of the rope and prepared to climb over the edge and into the boat. He pulled out his sword with one trembling hand. 'Remember, they're *only* fishermen, they're scared silly by Hooligans,' he reminded himself. 'What was it Gobber said to say when we went over the top? Oh I know, that stupid Hooligan War Cry – YAAAAH!'

'*Wait!*' whispered Hiccup, frantically scrambling up behind him. '*Don't do anything rash!*'

But it was too late.

Hiccup reached the top and Fishlegs threw himself over the side screaming 'Y-A-A-A-A-A-A-A-A-H!' at the top of his voice. Gobber really would have been proud of him.

Fishlegs landed on the deck, swinging his sword around his head in his most menacing and barbaric fashion, expecting to be faced by two or three terrified Peaceable fishermen.

Instead of which, three hundred and fifty of Rome's finest soldiers, heavily armed with the latest in modern weaponry, swivelled round to look at him.

'Oh *brother*…' whispered Hiccup to himself, still swinging from the rope and peering over the rim of the boat. 'So much for this being our lucky day…'

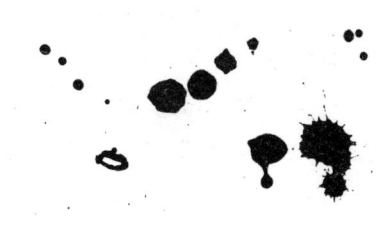

3. OUT OF THE COOKING POT AND INTO THE BARBECUE

'Uh-oh...' said Fishlegs.

This was most definitely NOT a Peaceable fishing boat.

It was, in fact, a sizeable Roman ship, seventy metres long from stern to prow. The sails were pure white, and high above, when Hiccup craned his neck, he could see the Roman flag of the Imperial Eagle flapping cheerily in the wind. The boat was crammed with what looked like an entire *legion* of Roman soldiers, who were now looking at Fishlegs with astonishment and fury.

There was a gigantic iron cage set near the mast of the boat.

An enormous number and variety of dragon species were being held prisoner behind the bars of this cage. Deadly Nadders, Flying 'Gators, Big Spotted Gormlesses, Yellow Vampires, Common-or-Gardens – you name it, they were all there, trapped together in a furious tangle of talons and wings and fangs, ready to be sent back to the restaurants and shoemakers in Rome.

'Oh, for Thor's sake,' whispered Hiccup. '*Roman Dragonrustlers*. I do not believe this…'

'Ah…' said Fishlegs with a nervous smile, backing towards the edge of the boat, 'I seem to have made some sort of *mistake*. This is the wrong boat, you see…' He tried to laugh in an airy fashion. 'So sorry to disturb… carry on with what you were doing why don't you…'

The nearest soldier, who was a six feet five centurion with legs like tree trunks, drew his sword with a nasty flourish.

'And where do you think you're going?' he asked Fishlegs in Latin*. He put out a big hand to grab Fishlegs and Fishlegs ducked under his arm in the nick of time.

'GET HIM!' yelled the big centurion and six or seven more soldiers made a leap towards Fishlegs.

Now, if Hiccup had been a traditional Hooligan Hero, he would have drawn his sword, Endeavour, and launched himself over the side to the aid of his

---

* Latin was the language spoken by the Ancient Romans. Most Vikings did not understand this language, but Hiccup had been secretly taught a little Latin by his grandfather, Old Wrinkly. 'Might come in useful,' Old Wrinkly had said. (As indeed it did, on occasions too numerous to mention.)

friend, shouting the Hooligan War Cry at the top of his voice.

But then if Hiccup had been a traditional Hooligan Hero, he would have been dead as a kipper several books ago. A *noble* kipper, perhaps, a gloriously *brave* kipper; but, nonetheless, a very, very dead kipper.

Instead, Hiccup sneaked over the edge of the boat as quietly as he could. As soft as a ghost, he hid behind a couple of jars of olive oil beside a bit of the deck that was covered by a large tent.

In the meantime, Fishlegs was being chased by the Roman soldiers. The chase didn't last long. Fishlegs ducked and dodged as best he could but finally ran into the stomach of a gigantic centurion who picked him clear off the ground.

'Look who we have here...' bellowed the centurion, as Fishlegs kicked his legs like a stranded beetle. 'A scary little Viking trying to attack us all on his own...'

'Har har har!' The other three hundred and forty-nine soldiers thought this was very funny.

'This is all a big mistake,' wailed Fishlegs, scratching himself violently as his eczema started coming out with the anxiety of the moment. 'Please let me go...'

'Let's take you to the Boss, little barbarian,' said the centurion. He carried Fishlegs over to the tent where Hiccup was hiding.

Hiccup peered out from behind his jar. Gently, he drew back the curtain so he could see what was happening.

Bright red in the face and trembling and itching, Fishlegs was brought before two richly dressed men reclining under the tent just a metre away from where Hiccup was crouching.

One of these men was very, very fat. So fat, that parts of his stomach were dripping over the edge of his couch and were being held up by a small slave. The other man was thin and wearing a fancy helmet with a gigantic plume and a face guard that covered his eyes.

The Fat Roman was eating nanodragons in honey from a plate on a low table in front of him. Nanodragons were a tiny species of dragon as

The Fat Consul ↘

numerous as insects. They were about the size of
locusts. The poor creatures were still alive and were
wriggling but unable to escape from the honey that
gummed up their wings. Hiccup could hear their
pathetic cries for help as the fat fingers picked them up
and gobbled them down.

The Fat Roman was difficult to understand
because he was talking with his mouth full.

'By Jupiter, Prefect,' drawled the Fat Roman
through a big helping of nanodragon. 'I do believe we
have been attacked by a teeny-weeny little barbarian...'

'So we have, Consul,' replied the Thin Prefect. 'I

The Thin Prefect

recognise this one. He is a member of one of the local Tribes I was telling you about. I'm worried that these Tribes might object to OUR FIENDISHLY CLEVER PLAN.'

'Oh yes, remind me what is our Fiendishly Clever Plan again?' asked the Fat Consul.

'One, disguise ourselves cunningly as Hooligans and kidnap the heir to the Brutish Bog-Burglars...'

'Marvellous,' spluttered the Fat Consul.

'Two,' said the Thin Prefect evilly, 'disguise ourselves cunningly as Bog-Burglers and kidnap the heir to the Hairy Hooligans...'

'You're a genius,' gurgled the Fat Consul.

'Three, the Bog-Burglars and the Hooligans are so busy fighting each other, they do not notice us STEALING EVERY SINGLE DRAGON IN THE INNER ISLES!'

'Bravo!' shouted the Fat Consul.

Hiccup would have loved to hang around and discover more about the plan. But he had important work to do. He had to get Fishlegs and himself off this ship alive.

Luckily, although everyday life as a Viking was a big struggle for Hiccup, he always came into his own

The Romans' Fiendishly Clever Plan

I The Romans disguise themselves cunningly as HOOLIGANS and kidnap the Heir to the BRUTISH BOG-BURGLARS...

II The Romans disguise themselves cunningly as BOG-BURGLARS and kidnap the Heir to the HAIRY HOOLIGANS...

III The BOG-BURGLARS and the HOOLIGANS are so busy fighting EACH OTHER they do not notice the Romans...Stealing EVERY SINGLE DRAGON IN THE WHOLE OF THE INNER ISLES!!!

Her her her her her (evil laughter)

in a crisis. And this sure was a crisis.

Hiccup quickly summed up the problem. On the other side: three hundred and fifty of Imperial Rome's finest soldiers armed with javelins, swords, spears, arrows, entrenching tools, etc etc etc. On his side: two scrawny Vikings and two small dragons, one on strike and one in a coma.

Yup, it was a crisis.

Hiccup's eye was caught by a tiny Electricsquirm clinging to the edge of the curtain. He looked from the Electricsquirm back to the cage of dragons. All that talk about distracting had given him an idea.

Perhaps *he* could use the Electricsquirm to distract the Romans' attention so that he could tiptoe up and open that cage of dragons. The dragons would rush out and attack everybody, and in the confusion, Hiccup could rescue Fishlegs...

Hiccup got out his handkerchief, wrapped it around his hand and picked up the Electricsquirm very, very carefully by the tail.

As its name suggests, the Electricsquirm gives a truly terrible electric shock if you touch it in the wrong place. The tail is fine, because it is made of some sort

The ELECTRICSQUIRM

This nanodragon is not aggressive, but it gives a truly terrible (although not fatal) electric shock when touched. Like their close cousins the Glow-worms, these creatures can be used as a source of light if no flame or candle is available.

~STATISTICS~

COLOURS: Transparent
SIZE: Very small
POISON: None..... 0
RADAR: None........ 0
ARMED WITH: Electricity......... 8
DEFENCE: Electricity....... 8
SPEED: Quite nippy..... 5
FEAR AND FIGHT FACTOR: Harmless if picked up by tail.... 5

Horny tail does not conduct electricity

of horny material that does not conduct electricity. But every other part of its body is likely to electrocute you.

Hiccup dropped to his hands and knees and softly pushed aside the curtains of the canopy.

The Thin Prefect and the Fat Consul were still deep in conversation.

The Fat Consul had nearly finished his nanodragons-in-honey. There was only one nanodragon left on the plate, struggling to escape. No one was looking at it; the two men were far too busy talking.

Hiccup crawled forwards, reached up and removed the nanodragon, putting it in his pocket. At least he had saved one of the poor creatures. He replaced the nanodragon with the Electricsquirm, which was almost exactly the same size.

Hiccup then crept away towards the cage of dragons.

Still talking, the Fat Consul reached out with one fat hand to grab another portion of nanodragon. His porky fingers scrabbled around in the honey for the final juicy morsel… and closed around the stomach of the Electricsquirm.

All thirty-eight stone of the Fat Consul soared quite one metre in the air.

His hair stuck up and out like a hedgehog, sparks flew out of his ears and his great blubbering mounds of flesh lit up with a strange blue light and quivered and shivered and wobbled and jiggled hysterically like a truly gigantic pink jelly that has been struck by lightning.

A few seconds later he fell to earth again. His toga turned to ashes around him and the vast flabby acres of his enormous stomach went on wobbling for the next ten minutes.

While everybody's attention was being drawn to the Fat Consul doing a one-man impression of the northern lights, Hiccup quietly lifted the wooden bar of the dragons' cage.

The next moment there was pandemonium aboard the deck of the Roman ship as the dragons poured out in a furious, shrieking, snapping and flaming river of beaks and wings and talons and tails, attacking the Romans, setting fire to the sails and causing no end of damage.

The Thin Prefect climbed on top of his couch in order to have a better view of what was happening.

'*Hiccup!*' he said to himself under his breath. 'This is the work of Hiccup Horrendous Haddock the

Third or I am a freshwater crayfish – which I'm not of course. Well, *I'll* flush you out of your hiding place, my fine fellow, you see if I don't… CENTURION!'

This command was directed at the Roman soldier who was still holding Fishlegs upside down by his left ankle.

'Prepare to execute the prisoner!'

The centurion drew his sword with a flourish and swung it up over his head.

'HIIIIIIIIIIIIIIIIIIIICUP!' screamed Fishlegs, absolutely terrified.

This was not part of Hiccup's plan.

'TOOOOOOOOOTHLESS!' screamed Hiccup.

4. TOOTHLESS TO THE RESCUE

Toothless had spent the last ten minutes muttering to himself at the top of the mast. At first he was so full of self-pity he had no time to worry about what was happening to his masters. 'NOBODY loves T-T-Toothless,' he said to himself. But then the noises from the Roman ship got louder, and the boys did not reappear, and he started to get worried.

When he heard Hiccup's YELL for help the little dragon called off his strike.

He zoomed off his perch and flew to the ship, and even from the height he was flying, his sharp little eyes immediately spotted that way down below on the deck there was a large Roman centurion who was holding Fishlegs by the leg. The centurion was about to execute Fishlegs with his sword.

Toothless folded his wings back and went into a dive, just as he might do if he were hunting mackerel or herring. His target was the centurion's head, and by the time he reached it, he was going so fast he was a little dragon blur. He tore into the helmet, sending feathers from the plume flying in all directions, and bit and scratched as hard as he could.

The centurion let out a yell of surprise and rage. For a moment he was knocked off balance, but he recovered when he realised his attacker was only a very small dragon. Fishlegs swung desperately from side to side, trying to break free; but the centurion was made of tough stuff. He tightened his grip on Fishlegs's ankle and swung his sword around, trying to hit Toothless with it.

So Hiccup grabbed a passing Slitherfang and shoved it up the centurion's tunic.

The centurion let out a bellow and dropped Fishlegs.

Wouldn't you?

A Slitherfang in the knickers is no laughing matter. The centurion hopped from foot to foot, clutching his bottom and squealing like a pig as he tried to catch hold of the nibbling, wriggling, scratching Slitherfang in his underwear.

'Let's get out of here!' howled Hiccup, hauling Fishlegs to his feet.

He also picked up a Roman helmet that was lying on the deck nearby. They were going to have some explaining to do to Gobber when they got back, and this might help.

A slitherfang in the KNICKERS is NO LAUGHING MATTER...

All around them there was chaos, with dragons attacking Romans and Romans attacking dragons and trying to put out the fires the dragons were making.

Hearts racing as fast as rabbits, panting and stumbling, Hiccup and Fishlegs ran as fast as they could to the spot where they had boarded the ship. The rope was still in place, *The Hopeful Puffin* would be waiting down below on the other side... Fishlegs got to the edge first, and scrambled over. Hiccup was only a few steps away from him... when a hand grabbed the back of his tunic, ripping out his pocket.

Hiccup's book, *How to Speak Dragonese*, fell on to the deck.

Hiccup stopped to reach down and pick it up...

... and came face to face with the glitteringly triumphant eyes of the Thin Prefect through the iron visor of his helmet. Hiccup's heart turned to ice. The Prefect was holding on to the other end of the book.

'AHA!' spat the Thin Prefect.

They both pulled. 'Let go!' hissed the Thin Prefect. 'You can't win, you know. This is mine now...' Hiccup could have let go but this was his book after all and despite his terror, some deep, indignant rage made him hang on strongly until…

… something sharp and iron shot out from beneath the Thin Prefect's cloak and cut into the back of Hiccup's hand.

Hiccup screamed and jumped backwards.

The book split in two and before the Thin Prefect could pull himself together and catch hold of him again Hiccup scrambled away and over the edge of the ship.

There wasn't even time to climb down the rope. Hiccup swung from it, and then let go, crashing on to the deck of *The Hopeful Puffin* some way below.

Fishlegs cut the rope that tied them to the ship, and their little boat was pulled away so swiftly by the current that she went into one of her spins.

'Where's Toothless?' asked Hiccup.

Toothless had been held up.

His foot was caught in the centurion's chin-strap, and for a moment they were tied together – and Toothless had quite a bumpy ride because the centurion was jumping up and down like an octopus with chicken pox, as he tried to get rid of the Slitherfang in his knickers.

Toothless finally snapped the chin-strap with his hard little gums and to Hiccup's relief, as *The Hopeful Puffin* twirled around for the fifth time – looking for all the world as if she was dancing – Toothless came screeching up to the edge of the ship towards them at the speed of a flying arrow.

'Oh, thank Thor!' Hiccup exclaimed joyfully.

But one minute Toothless was flying through the air like a stormy petrel in a hurry; the next a net weighted with stones appeared out of nowhere, wrapped itself round the little dragon in midair and brought him back down on to the deck of the Roman ship as if struck by a spear.

'TOOOOOOOOTHLESS!' cried Hiccup.

Two figures appeared over the edge of the ship. One was the Thin Prefect holding half of the *How to Speak Dragonese* book. The other was a Roman soldier. In one hand he held a trident. In the other he held a net...

... and within that net, struggling and biting and turning wild somersaults in his desperation to be free, was...

… Toothless.

The Hopeful Puffin made another crazy turn and Hiccup gazed at his captured dragon in despair until the Roman ship was swallowed up by the fog and Hiccup could see him no more.

How to Speak Dragonese

by

Hiccup Horrendous Haddock III

DraGon VocaBulary

Pishyou	please
Thankee	thank you
Munch-munch	eat
Crappa Cack-cack	poo
Dobbli wobbli ⎫ Botti Bum ⎭	bottom
No like it	I don't like it
Me like it	I do like it
Gobba	spit
Botty-crackers ⎫ Buttok-thunder ⎬ Smelly breezers ⎭	farts
Hoosus	house
Gaff	nest
Chuck-it-up ⎫ Wobble-di-guts ⎭	to be sick
Yum-yum on di bum	to bite someone on the bottom
Yum-yum on di tum	to bite someone on the stomach
Yum-yum on di thumb	to bite someone on the finger
Miaowla	cat

Bathtime

When a dragon has spent the whole day in a mud wallow and they then want to curl up in your bed you have no option. YOU HAVE TO GIVE THEM A BATH. Good luck.

Dragon: Me na wash di bum. Me na wash di face. Me na wash di claws. Me na splishy oo di splashy ATALL *I do not want a bath*

You are going to have to be cunning and use PSYCHOLOGY

You: Na bathtime ever never ever never. Me repeeti. Na bathtime EVER NEVER. *On no account are you to get in the bath*

Dragon (whining): Me wanti splishy splashy
You: Okey dokey just wun time. *All right just this once*

Hoody drunken di bath juice? *Who has drunk up the bath water?*

DraGon Vocabulary

Dim-woof	dog
Squeaky-snack	mouse
Pestistings	nanodragons
Randifloss	rabbits
Stink-fish	haddock
Prickle-burger	a deer
Scrumlush	delicious
Doubly yuck-yuck	disgusting
Bum-support	chair
Sleepy-Slab	bed
Munchy-holder	table

Warmadi-tootsies	fire
Do di girly hoo-hoo	burst into tears
Do di wobbly screamers	to have a tantrum
Do di chuckli ha-has	to laugh
Frieundlee	friend
Piss-people	enemy
Do di sereemi beserkers	
Do di hissi fittings	} to lose your temper
Do di heehi jeebys	

Dinner time

Dragon: Issa yuck-yuck
This is disgusting

Dragon: Me na likeit di stinkfish. Issa yuck-yuck.
Issa poo-poo. Issa doubly doubly yuck-yuck.
*I don't like haddock. It's revolting. It's gross. It's
really revolting*

You: Okey dokey so questa yow eaty?
*Alright then, so what **will** you eat?*

Dragon: Me eaty di miaowla...
I want to eat the cat...

You: (you can raise your voice now) NA EATY
DI BUM-SUPPORT, NA EATY DI SLEEPY-SLAB
PLUS DOUBLY DOUBLY NA EATY DI
MIAOWLA!
*Don't eat the chair, don't eat the bed and definitely
don't eat the cat!*

draGon vocabulary

Do di yucky gobba-hath	
Swappa da yucki	to kiss
lip-juice	
Do di vomit-belly	
squeezes	to hug
Do di scarlet strokings	to scratch
'es alright reely	to love

Da wingless	
Land prisoners	
Skyless dirt grubbers	humans
No brainers	
Flicka-flame	to set fire to
Snotting-gum	Winkles
Brain-goo	snot
Smelly-breezers	farts

Talking to BIG DraGoNS

Dragon: ooohscrumplush yum-yuminditum eatings di ickle prickle-burger!
'Ooh delicious a scrummy little Viking!'

You: Me look a di scrummy may me ow-in-di-tummy
'I may look delicious but I'm actually very poisonous'

And if that doesn't work...

You: Me gambla yow na flicka-flame di gaff da di pesti-stings
'I bet you can't set fire to that nanodragon nest'
Dragon: Easipeasilemonsqueezi
'I can do that no problem'

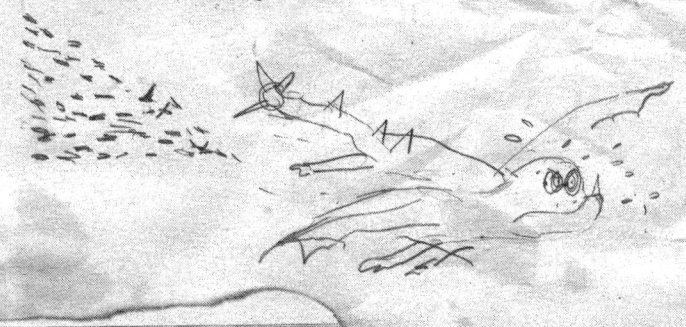

I hate Snotlout

GOBBER
is a
girly

5. BACK ON BERK

By the time *The Hopeful Puffin* had stopped turning round in circles, the fog had started to lift a little. Half an hour later, the mist had vanished entirely, and they could see for miles in every direction.

The Roman ship was nowhere to be seen.

The water was as cold as ice again, so there was no further danger of bumping into any Sharkworms. They had not gone as far off course as Hiccup had thought. They set off towards the distant silhouette of Berk to the north. Fishlegs took the rudder because Hiccup was too depressed to do anything.

Hiccup sat staring at his half of *How to Speak Dragonese*. All that work, all that time spent dragonwatching at the Wild Dragon Cliff, ripped in two. He was trying not to think of what might be happening to Toothless on board the Roman ship.

Toothless hated the idea of being trapped so much Hiccup even had to leave the door open when they went to bed. And now there he was, most likely locked up in that horrible iron cage.

We'd just had an argument, too, thought Hiccup in total misery. *And he flew to our rescue… and now I might never see him again.*

Horrorcow finally woke up from her deep sleep. 'Did you get that helmet?' she yawned.

'Not exactly,' replied Fishlegs grimly. 'It's a long story.'

In her strange, spinning and zigzagging fashion, *The Hopeful Puffin* drew nearer to the little Isle of Berk.

The Isle of Berk has been home to the Hooligan Tribes for so long as to seem like for ever. It is one of the smallest inhabited islands in the Barbaric Archipelago, and perhaps the best way to describe it is 'wet'. There are twenty-eight words for 'rain' in the Hooligan language. And Berk is the kind of place where the sea is always wandering up on to the land. Even at the Highest Point you can find scallop shells and dolphins' bones, thrown up by some gigantic tide or storm.

So, what with the rain pouring down constantly from above, and the sea sneaking up from below, the Hooligans spend most of their lives up to their knees in muddy saltwater.

As they got nearer to Berk they didn't have time to feel sorry for themselves. *The Hopeful Puffin* was in difficulties. Never a *very* sea-worthy boat, she had taken two big knocks, first when she was rammed by Snotlout's boat *Sparrowhawk*, then when Hiccup jumped down on to her decks from the Roman ship. She was taking on water even faster than normal.

Despite Hiccup and Fishlegs bailing out the water as quickly as they could with their helmets, by the time they reached Hooligan Harbour, she sank entirely.

They had to swim the last hundred metres, Hiccup holding Fishlegs up, because (unusually for a Viking) Fishlegs had never quite mastered the doggy paddle.

To make matters worse, Gobber was standing on the harbour wall watching them come in, arms folded, brows as low as Thor's thunderclouds. When *The Hopeful Puffin* disappeared beneath the water he looked as if he might explode.

'It hasn't been a very successful day, has it?' moaned Fishlegs as they struggled out of the sea and on to the rocks. 'At least we didn't meet any Sharkworms, after all…'

GOBBER was not amused.

'I'm not sure there ever *were* any Sharkworms,' said Hiccup through gritted teeth. He looked back sadly at the three circles of ripples and bubbles that were all that remained of *The Hopeful Puffin*. She had never been the most beautiful of boats but to him she was the best.

Slipping and sliding on the seaweedy rocks, they clambered reluctantly towards Gobber and stood before him, soaking wet, heads bowed. Fishlegs timidly offered him the Roman helmet.

Gobber was not amused.

'WHAT,' he bellowed, pointing furiously at the Roman helmet, 'WHAT in the name of Woden is *this?*'

'A Roman helmet, sir,' admitted Fishlegs. 'We sort of accidentally boarded a Roman ship *by mistake…* we got lost you see, sir…'

'You got LOST?' boomed Gobber, not believing his ears. 'Vikings don't get LOST. And how could you possibly board a Roman ship by mistake? A Roman ship doesn't look anything like a Peaceable fishing boat!'

'Yes I know, sir,' stammered Fishlegs. 'But we thought there were these Sharkworms you see—'

'And WHERE,' Gobber interrupted Fishlegs, his voice dangerously calm, 'WHERE is your boat?'

'Ah, yes, well,' said Fishlegs miserably. 'The boat sort of sank, sir.'

'THE BOAT SORT OF SANK?' roared Gobber. 'YOU CALL YOURSELVES VIKINGS AND YOU SORT OF SINK YOUR OWN BOAT ON A PERFECTLY CALM DAY TWO HUNDRED METRES FROM YOUR OWN ISLAND? WHAT KIND OF HOOLIGANS ARE YOU, ANYWAY? YOU CAN'T BUILD BOATS, YOU CAN'T TRAIN DRAGONS, FISHLEGS HERE CAN'T EVEN SWIM...'

'Saltwater brings out my eczema...' mumbled Fishlegs.

'YOU'RE SUPPOSED TO BE A PIRATE!' howled Gobber. 'AS IT IS, YOU ARE THE MOST USELESS, MISERABLE, PATHETIC EXCUSES FOR TADPOLE POOS I HAVE EVER MET IN

MY ENTIRE LIFE! I AM LOST FOR WORDS...'

Despite being lost for words, Gobber yelled at them for the next ten minutes, telling them they were a disgrace to their Tribe and the worst recruits he had ever had. He put them on limpet rations for the next three weeks, and said the next time anything like this happened they would be expelled from the Programme.

At home, it wasn't much better.

During supper, Hiccup explained to his father about the unfortunate accident of boarding the Roman galley by mistake, and about the kidnapping of Toothless, and how the Prefect had got hold of half of *How to Speak Dragonese*, and how Stoick really should send a war party to rescue Toothless and the book. Hiccup showed the sad remains of *How to Speak Dragonese* and the Roman helmet to his father to prove his story was genuine.

'Mmmmmmm,' said Stoick thoughtfully. Stoick was a great giant of a man with enough red, haystacky beard and barrels of belly to kit out at least *two* decent-sized Viking chieftains.

He wasn't really concentrating, because he was reading Hiccup's Pirate Training report, which was the worst report he had ever read. *Thumbnails of Thor*, he was thinking, *how can* anybody *get –4 for Advanced Rudery?* And nothing at all for Beginner Burping and Hammerthrowing Studies, which had been Stoick's favourite subjects when HE was a boy.

Stoick was trying very hard not to feel disappointed in his son. He kept telling himself that Hiccup was just a slow developer, and would soon start getting muscles and nose hair, and scoring the winning goal in Bashyball games like Stoick had himself. But what was he *doing*, earning reports like 'Hiccup is the worst sailor I have ever taught in twenty years'? How could he have come back from a perfectly straightforward training exercise having misplaced both his dragon *and* his boat? And how could he *possibly* have got lost and accidentally boarded a Roman ship rather than a Peaceable fishing boat?

Vikings didn't get lost.

Stoick opened his mouth to bellow at his son.

And then he closed it again.

Small, skinny, freckled and unsatisfactory, Hiccup's worried face looked up at him. He was clearly desperately anxious about that laughably tiny dragon of his. Stoick didn't have the heart to be angry. He crumpled up the report in one gigantic fist.

Berk Pirate
Training Programme
REPORT CARD

Name of child: *Hiccup H.H. III*

SUBJECT	Teacher's Report	Mark out of 10
BEGINNER BURPING	Hiccup cannot get up the necessary wind to do well in this subject.	0/10 GOBBER
FRIGHTENING FOREIGNERS	Must stop speaking in impeccable French and work on his yelling..	1/10 GOBBER
ADVANCED RUDERY	@*!*!*!	-4/10 GOBBER
HAMMERTHROWING STUDIES	Might improve when he can actually pick up the hammer.	0/10 RUGGED RITA
SWORDFIGHTING LESSONS	Quick reflexes and strong fancy footwork. I'm impressed. Needs to work on his aggression.	9/10 GORMLESS THE GRIM
SHIPBUILDING	I have grave doubts that the Hopeful Puffin will float.	0/10 GOBBER
BOARDING AN ENEMY SHIP	Hiccup is the worst sailor I have ever taught in twenty years.	HA! HA! HA! GOBBER
BASHYBALL	Spends most of his time in the mud being sat on.	1/10 GOBBER

STOICK the VAST
reading Hiccup's report

'Son,' he said gently and gravely, 'I am sorry
you have lost Ruthless—'

'Toothless!' Hiccup interrupted indignantly.
'He's called Toothless.'

'Toothless,' Stoick corrected himself hurriedly.
'But I am about to tell you something very important.'

Stoick took Hiccup by the shoulders and
looked him in the eyes. 'You,' he said solemnly, 'are
the son of a Chief. You have lost your pet, but you
must be brave. You must be a MAN about it. There

will be other dragons…'

'Not like Toothless!' objected Hiccup, in distress. 'That dragon trusted me and I let him down!'

'Silence!' said Stoick sternly. 'What does a Chief feel, son?'

'A Chief feels no pain,' replied Hiccup obediently. 'But Father—'

Stoick was just getting into his stride. 'A Chief feels no pain. A Chief feels no fear. A Chief must be above mere weak, personal feelings. There is no question of putting together a War Party to rescue your dragon. It would be a waste of our warriors' time. The Romans are probably halfway back to Rome by now and they'll have turned Useless into a handbag—'

'Toothless,' corrected Hiccup again, 'and that's what I'm telling you, Father, I overheard them talking and I think they're not just passing through.'

'Talking?' roared Stoick, his eyebrows lowering. 'What do you mean TALKING? How did you understand these Romans?'

'Ah,' admitted Hiccup. 'Old Wrinkly's been teaching me some Latin, you see—'

'Latin? LATIN?' Stoick exploded. He crashed his fist so hard on the table that the oysters they'd been tucking in to did a couple of cartwheels in the air. 'My son, my son, has been speaking LATIN!'

He controlled himself with an effort. 'Hooligans do not, I repeat, DO NOT, speak Latin. What are they teaching you in your Frightening Foreigners lessons? When a Hooligan meets a foreigner he shouts at it loudly and slowly. That's the only language a foreigner understands. Hooligans don't talk to dragons either. Or write books about them. You're spending far too much time scribbling about dragons and not enough time preparing to become a Chief.'

Stoick took the half of *How to Speak Dragonese* out of Hiccup's hands and threw it on to the fire. Hiccup gasped. That book had everything he had ever learned about dragons in it. How would he ever talk to dragons again without it?

Stoick stomped off.

As soon as he was out of sight, Hiccup burned his fingers pulling the book out of the flames. Luckily it was still quite damp, and the edges were only very slightly burnt.

That night, for the first time in a long, long

while,
Hiccup had to
go to bed without the
company of Toothless. The little dragon was a small,
wriggling, snoring hot-water bottle. Now Hiccup lay
awake till the early hours of the morning, shivering
uncontrollably under the thin covers, his feet and
hands as cold as the North Pole, his ears trembling in
the icy draught. And when eventually he slipped in
and out of a feverish sleep, the nightdragons and the
wind and the wolves seemed to be howling all
together, 'You've lost Tooooothlesss! Lost him for
ever! Lost Tooooooothless! Lost him
foreverandeverandever' over and over and over again.

6. THAT NIGHT IN SINISTER ROMAN FORT SINISTER

Far, far away from Berk in the sinister Fort Sinister, there was a dungeon so deep beneath sea level that no light ever reached it, a dungeon so far away that even the gods had forgotten it existed.

Toothless, who was afraid of the dark and of small spaces, lay in utter blackness in a cage so cramped he could hardly turn over.

He was crying.

'H-h-help,' whimpered poor Toothless in a voice he knew could not be heard.

'H-h-h-h-help.'

"H-h-help" whispered Toothless, in a voice he knew could not be heard. "H-h-help...'"

7. THE NANODRAGON

Hiccup woke very early. He had just been having a lovely dream about playing a tickling game with Toothless and he woke up laughing. For a moment everything was all right again and he forgot Toothless had gone and reached out for him, only to feel the chilly, damp depression in the bed where Toothless should have been. He was instantly miserable again, and lay, teeth chattering, under the bedclothes trying to get up the willpower to brave the cold and get dressed in the still-slightly-damp-and-salty clothes he was wearing yesterday. He gradually became aware that what had woken him was a very faint and tiny singing noise, a reedy little sound like the wind caught in a cowrie shell, but with an edge of menace to it.

The song went something like this:

SONG OF THE NANODRAGON (while licking off honey)

O Human Fatness who tried to eat me
Great Wobbling Vomit of Repulsive Man-Flesh
I cannot kill you NOW
Though I would like to
But you will regret this, Blubber-Man
You will regret this in the quiet darkness of the night-time
For I have friends
I have friends who will itch you into nightmares
Their feet will plough your skin into rashes
And you will sleep no more, o Stomach-with-a-Head-on-it
You will sleep no more

O Balloon of Lard who tried to eat me
Man Uglier than an Exploded Jellyfish
I cannot kill you NOW
Though I would like to
But I can wait, Flesh-Dangler
I can wait, ticking in the corner like Fate
And I have friends
I have friends who will crawl with me into your coffin
Where you are lying, hoping for the quiet sleep of Death
And we will eat YOU, o Sad Lump of Man Meat
We will eat you

Where was the song coming from?

Eventually, Hiccup realised the noise seemed to be sneaking out of the jacket he had worn the day before and left to dry on the back of a chair in front of the fire.

And then he remembered the nanodragon he had replaced with the Electricsquirm and put in his pocket.

Hiccup braced himself against the cold, jumped out of bed, dragged his clothes on, and approached the jacket. Carefully, he put his hand into the pocket and drew it out again with a gasp. Not only was there a yucky warm mess of honey in there, but the nanodragon had bitten him on the end of his finger.

As Hiccup put the finger in his mouth (you should always do this with a nanodragon bite – it helps to draw out the sting) the nanodragon flew out of the pocket, fluttered around the room, and landed on the window-sill.

The nanodragon had spent the night cleaning the sticky honey off his body with his tongue. He was a handsome little beast. No bigger than a grasshopper, he was a gleaming rust-red with flecks of charcoal, and the morning sun shone through his gossamer-thin wings and threw red and black spots all round the room.

Something about the self-importance of the little animal, the arrogance with which he held himself, made Hiccup ask, 'Who are you?'

'I,' squeaked the tiny creature grandly, 'am the Centre of the Universe.'

Hiccup looked carefully at the very small animal in front of him. 'You ARE?' he said, polite but amazed. 'You mean you are Thor or Woden in disguise?'

'Thor and Woden!' snorted the creature derisively. 'Fairy stories! No, I am Ziggerastica the Living God.'

Hiccup looked blank.

'Most High and Mighty Ruler of the Nano Empire. Despot of the Northern Grasses...'

Hiccup shook his head regretfully.

Ziggerastica

'You MUST know about me!' piped Ziggerastica. 'Great Scourge of the Bracken Dwellers... Doesn't that ring any bells at all?'

'Nope,' said Hiccup. 'I'm so sorry. I've never heard of you before.'

'I don't know, you Humans,' fumed Ziggerastica, hugely offended. 'Ignorant as well as ugly.'

'I'm not ugly,' protested Hiccup. 'That is a very rude thing to say.'

Ziggerastica wasn't listening. 'You're so caught up in your own world that you never bother to lower your fat noses to the ground and have a look at what's going on in the Real World! Well, Boy-With-a-Face-like-a-Stinky-Haddock, you have had the good fortune to save the life of the most Powerful Being in the Galaxy...'

'If you're the most Powerful Being in the Galaxy,' said Hiccup, 'how come you didn't get your nanodragons to come and save you from the big Fat Roman?'

'Even a Living God has his weak spots,' replied Ziggerastica. 'And mine happens to be honey. I love the stuff. But the nanodragon cry for help is created by rubbing the back legs together, and honey gums up the noise... It is delicious, though... However, the point is, that since you have saved my life, I am honour-bound to save yours in return, however huge and stinking and Wingless you are...'

'Thank you,' murmured Hiccup.

'... with an ugly nose,' added the creature, 'and those brown marks that look like spots—'

'Those are freckles!' said Hiccup indignantly.

'They are not nice,' said Ziggerastica. 'They displease my eye. But the Living God does not forget a debt. In mortal danger you just have to say the word Ziggerastica and I shall come to your aid...'

And what on earth could someone as small as YOU do? Hiccup thought to himself, but it would have been rude to say it. 'How will you hear me?' he asked instead.

The nanodragon ignored the question.

'Just say the word Ziggerastica and I will come. However, be warned... You can call on my Most Glorious Aid just once, and once alone. When I have repaid my debt you will become just another smelly, repellent human to me. So choose your time wisely, Boy-with-Spots-on-his-Ugly-Nose, choose your time wisely...'

And with that the rude little animal gave a last shake of his wings and flew out of the window.

Hiccup wasn't quite sure what to make of this conversation. It seemed unlikely that a creature as small as Ziggerastica could be as powerful as he seemed to think he was. *But on the other hand, I need all the help I can get,* Hiccup thought gloomily.

At breakfast, Hiccup was more miserable than he had ever been in his life. He couldn't eat a thing. He just sat there pushing his kipper sadly round his plate. His grandfather, Old Wrinkly, tried to ask him what the matter was, but Hiccup just sighed.

'What does a Chief feel?' asked Stoick the Vast, seeing his son drooping.

'A Chief feels no pain, Father,' replied Hiccup glumly.

In the middle of the meal a Carrier Dragon flew in the window, dropped a letter addressed to Stoick on the table, and flew out again.

The letter was from Big-Boobied Bertha, the chief of the Bog-Burglars. The Bog-Burglars were a

tribe of particularly fearsome female warriors who
lived on an island some way to the west of the Isle of
Berk. (Please see map at the beginning of this book.)
The Hooligans had a long-running feud with the Bog-
Burglars which had started many, many years ago,
when the Bog-Burglars stole the shield of Hiccup's
great-great-grandfather, Grimbeard the Ghastly.

Hiccup read the letter over Stoick's shoulder.

*Greetings You Fat Burglar, I see you have broken the truce
we have had for so many years and wish to make war with us
again... how dare you steal the noble Heir to the Bog-Burglar
Tribe? You are a thief and I give you two weeks to return our
Heir to us unharmed... otherwise I shall declare a blood feud
and we will sail to Berk in all our strength and exterminate the
lot of you... it should be easy peasy – you Hooligans always
did fight like a load of bunny rabbits... Yours very untruly,
Bertha, Chief of the Bog-Burglars.*

Stoick grew more and more purple in the face as he
read the letter. Finally, he came to the end and with a
roar he tore the paper up into little pieces and
stamped on them.

He was hopping mad. Stoick was often batey,

I Declare a BLOOD FEUD!!

often shouty, often going off the deep end. But this time he lost his temper.

And when a Hooligan loses his temper, he REALLY loses it. A Hooligan in a rage yells so loudly it makes his ordinary yelling sound like a baby's lullaby.

'I DECLARE A BLOOD FEUD!' yelled Stoick the Vast.

'Oh, *brother*.' Hiccup raised his eyes to the heavens. 'I do not believe this… this is all we need! Hang on a minute, Father, let's stay calm here. I really don't think this was from the Bog-Burglars. We haven't *got* their Heir have we? So SOMEONE ELSE must have stolen her. I overheard the Romans saying they would *pretend* to be the Bog-Burglars so they can get us to fight *each other*.'

'YOU STAY OUT OF THIS, HICCUP!' roared Stoick the Vast. 'POLITICS IS FOR GROWN-UPS! FETCH ME MY SWORD! SOUND THE WAR HORNS! I WANT EVERY MAN, WOMAN AND CHILD PRACTISING THEIR SWORDFIGHTING NIGHT AND DAY FOR THE NEXT TWO WEEKS!'

'But, Father,' protested Hiccup, '*please* use your head here—'

Blood Feud Table

Vikings were always fighting each other. Here is a table to explain the current state of blood-feuds. Like all these tables, it will probably confuse you even more than you were already.

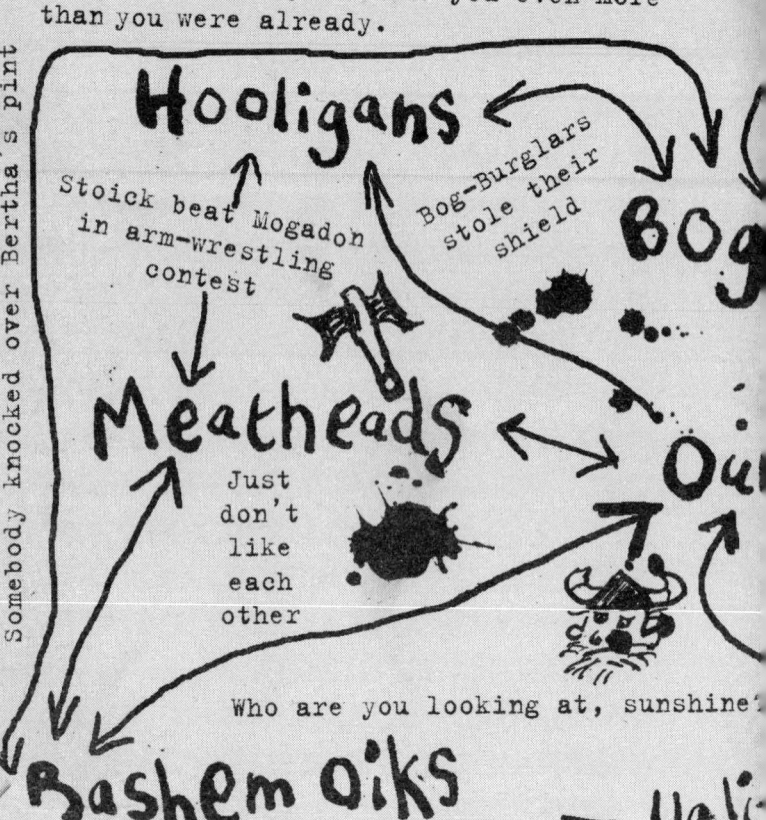

Hooligans

Stoick beat Mogadon in arm-wrestling contest

Bog-Burglars stole their shield

Bog

Meatheads

Just don't like each other

Ou

Somebody knocked over Bertha's pint

Who are you looking at, sunshine?

Bashem Oiks

Ugli

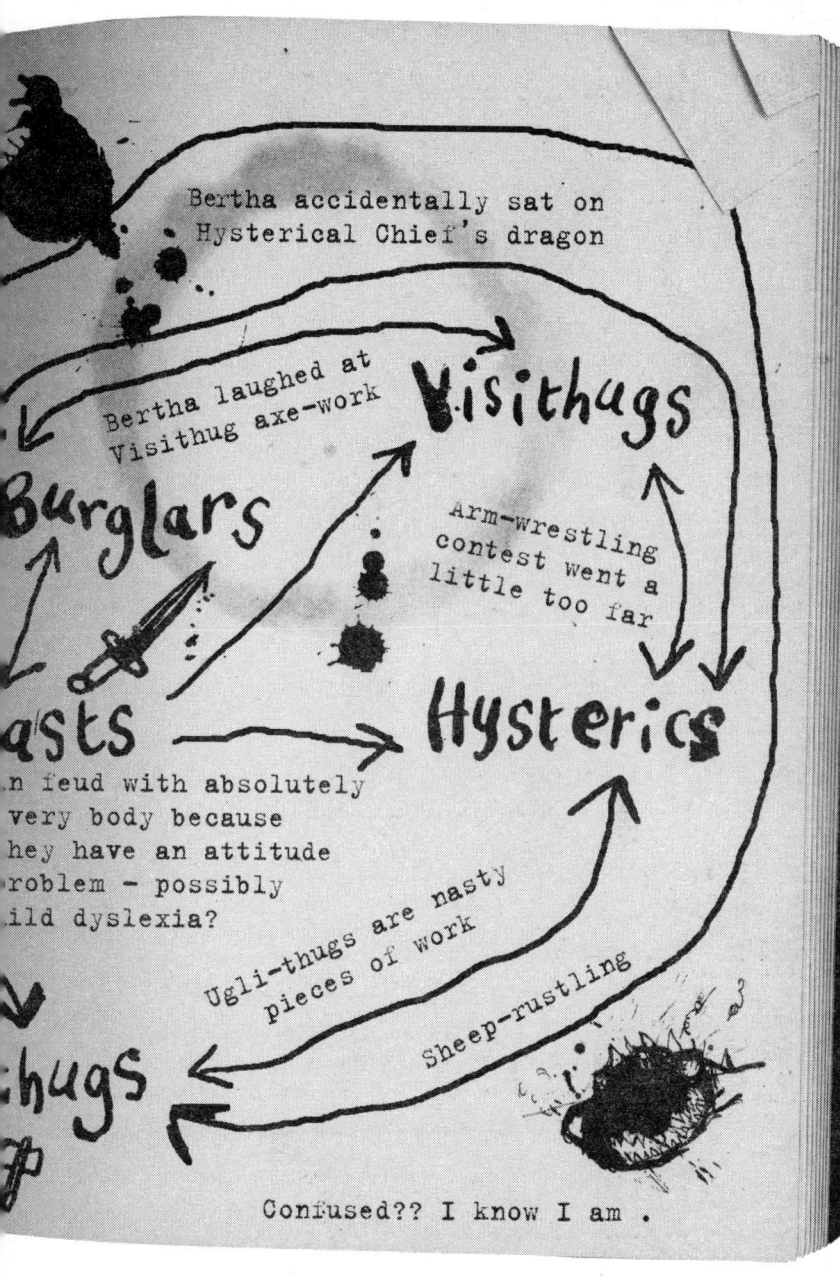

Bertha accidentally sat on Hysterical Chief's dragon

Bertha laughed at Visithug axe-work

Visithugs

Burglars

Arm-wrestling contest went a little too far

...asts

Hysterics

...n feud with absolutely
...very body because
...hey have an attitude
...roblem — possibly
...ild dyslexia?

Ugli-thugs are nasty pieces of work

Sheep-rustling

...thugs

Confused?? I know I am .

'I AM USING MY HEAD!' roared Stoick the Vast, headbutting the wall. 'IF THOSE BOG-BURGLARS SET ONE *TOE* INTO HOOLIGAN WATERS, BY THOR, THEY'RE GOING TO REGRET IT!'

Hiccup could feel himself getting cross too. He didn't stand up to his father very often but he was so upset about Toothless that he got up and stood in front of Stoick with his hands on his hips.

'Why don't you BELIEVE ME?' he asked furiously. 'I have *told* you and *told* you, this is the work of the ROMANS. I have even brought you back a Roman helmet to prove it.'

Hiccup pointed to the Roman helmet, which was sitting on a stool in the corner of the room. 'We COULD send out a War Party to go and find these Romans, and Toothless too… but oh *no*, you would rather stay here beating up the Bog-Burglars than believe the word of your OWN SON…'

For a moment it seemed as if Hiccup was getting through to his father. Stoick's nostrils stopped flaring and he ceased to paw the ground with his foot.

He looked at the Roman helmet. Maybe, just maybe, Hiccup was right…

But then he looked at Big-Boobied Bertha's letter and his temper returned.

'THE ONLY GOOD BOG-BURGLAR IS A DEAD BOG-BURGLAR!' shouted Stoick at the top of his voice, and he stalked out of the room.

'Don't blame your father too much, will you, Hiccup?' said Old Wrinkly sadly. 'He means well, but when things get complicated, he gets confused. By the way, aren't you going to be late for your Frightening Foreigners lesson?'

'Oh my goodness,' said Hiccup. 'So I am…'

8. THE FRIGHTENING FOREIGNERS LESSON

It was a glorious, blue, breezy day but Hiccup had no time to admire it. He ran as fast as he could towards the Great Hall where the Frightening Foreigners

lesson was being held. Gobber hadn't arrived yet, so the young barbarians were making a gigantic racket. Sharpknife and Tuffnut Junior were having a swordfight in one corner. The boys' dragons were lying in front of the gigantic fire, snapping and snarling at each other. Snotlout and Dogsbreath the Duhbrain were sitting on Fishlegs while Fireworm set fire to a pile of Fishlegs's workbooks.

'Why don't you pick on someone your own size, you brainless brutes?' snapped Hiccup at the bullies, putting out the fire with his jacket.

'Thanks, Hiccup,' panted Fishlegs.

'Well, well, *well*,' drawled Snotlout, removing his knee from Fishlegs's stomach and sauntering over to where Hiccup was sitting.

'Some Vikings you two are! I hear you couldn't even tell the difference between a Peaceable fishing boat and a seventy-metre Roman ship, and you have got to be the first pirates EVER to sink their *own* boat...'

'Har har har har,' laughed all the other boys.

'And most pathetic of all,' jeered Snotlout, 'you lost your ridiculous fangless microbe of a dragon.'

'Some loss,' sneered Fireworm, sharpening her claws on Hiccup's helmet with an acutely unpleasant scritching noise. 'That creature was a disgrace to us green-blooded FireBrothers of the Snake.'

'Toothless was a fine, fine dragon,' said Hiccup quietly, trying to keep his temper.

'He was a HOPELESS dragon,' mocked Snotlout. 'Never mind, Hiccup. He'll make a much better Roman handbag—'

'YOU TAKE THAT BACK, YOU SNOT-FACED, SNOT-NOSED, ELEPHANT-NOSTRILLED, BOTTOM-BRAINED BULLY!' yelled Hiccup.

The door opened with a gigantic crash.

'Excellent Advanced Rudery, Hiccup!' roared Gobber the Belch. 'We'll make a Viking of you yet!'

'I hope you don't mind, sir,' spat Snotlout, advancing on Hiccup with his fists raised and a nasty look in his eye, 'if I just kill him for that one…'

'But I do mind,' said Gobber. 'This is a Frightening Foreigners lesson, not a free-for-all – SIDDOWN *NOW* YOU 'ORRIBLE LITTLE

EXCUSES FOR VIKINGS!'

The boys scrambled for their places on the floor at Gobber's feet. Even Snotlout knew better than to disobey Gobber, and he sat down too, muttering darkly to Hiccup that he would get him later.

'This lesson is all about Taking Money with Menaces,' yelled Gobber. 'HICCUP! WARTIHOG! Stand up here in the front. Hiccup, I want *you* to be the Hooligan Invader and Wartihog to be the simple Gaulish farmer. What Terrifying Techniques can you use to get Wartihog's belongings?'

Hiccup got to his feet, but he wasn't really concentrating.

'*Excusez-moi, mon brave,*' said Hiccup absent-mindedly. '*Mais pouvez-vous me donner votre—*'

Wartihog bashed him.

'OH FOR THOR'S SAKE, HICCUP!' exploded Gobber bateily. 'I TAKE BACK WHAT I SAID A MOMENT AGO! HAVE I TAUGHT YOU NOTHING? VIKINGS DON'T TALK IN SILLY FOREIGN LANGUAGES, THEY YELL, HICCUP, YELL!'

Gobber controlled himself with an effort. 'Sit down, Hiccup. Snotlout, show PATHETIC Hiccup how to perform this *perfectly simple* exercise.'

Two seconds later, to great cheers of 'BRAVO!' from Gobber and the rest of the class, Snotlout had Wartihog in a Baggybum Bearhug and was removing not only his money but also his helmet, jacket and trousers.

Gobber put his hands on his hips, threw back his huge hairy head until the horns on his helmet touched the wall behind him, and shouted with laughter.

'YOU SEE, HICCUP?' he bellowed in between great guffaws. 'THAT'S HOW TO FRIGHTEN A FOREIGN—'

The door flew open.

Two enormous, masked Kidnappers crashed into the room with yells that froze the blood and made the hairs on Hiccup's head stand up like the spines on a sea-urchin. They were dressed in traditional Bog-Burglar costume but it was obvious to Hiccup that this was a couple of Roman soldiers in not a very good disguise. For starters Bog-Burglar soldiers were always women. But these were clearly big hairy muscly men in dresses with pigs' bladders stuffed down their blouses instead of bosoms.

The First Kidnapper was holding a couple of double-headed axes the size of dinner plates and he threw one of these as hard as he could in Gobber's direction. The axe flew through the air, missed Gobber's head by a hair's-breadth, and pinned him to the wall by his beard.

'AAAAAAAAAAAARGH!' gurgled Gobber, unable to move and gazing at the shining blade less than a centimetre from his nose.

'HE WHO IS MOVING, PLEASE, LOSES ZE HEAD, AND ZE DRAGONS ALSO,' yelled the First Kidnapper, speaking very badly in Norse* and swinging the other axe round his head.

Not a boy or a dragon moved.

'Okey-dokey, please,' continued the First Kidnapper in a quieter voice. 'Give us what we is wantings and nobody she gets hurt. *Which one of you lots is being the Heir to the Hairy Hooligans?*'

Everyone was silent.

'No make me get cross, please…' warned the First Kidnapper.

'You no like her when she is cross,' said the

---

* Norse is the language all Vikings speak.

second one, fingering his axe lovingly.

'Just tell me… WHO IS BEING THE HEIR TO THE HAIRY HOOLIGANS?'

Nobody answered them and now they started talking to each other in Latin.

'OK, Marcus,' the First Kidnapper said to the Second Kidnapper.

'They're not telling, but the Boss said the Heir to the Hairy Hooligans is a weedy-looking kid – which one is he, then?'

The Second Kidnapper pointed at Hiccup. 'It must be that one with the red hair,' he said. 'Look at him, he's got arms like spaghetti!'

'But what about the one with the face like a haddock?' objected the First Kidnapper, indicating Fishlegs. 'That's got to be the weediest-looking kid I've ever seen in my life…'

'Oooh it's a toughie,' said the Second Kidnapper. 'I think we have to take them both, just in case. If we get it wrong the Boss will be cross, and you know what he's like when he's cross…'

So the Second Kidnapper picked up both Hiccup and Fishlegs and put them over his shoulders.

'You must be doing countings to a thousands before you is leavings this room,' the First Kidnapper warned the class of open-mouthed Viking boys. 'Or we be killings these boys! You be tellings your Chief that Big-Boobied Bertha sends you her lovings and is giving you this letter.'

The Kidnappers handed Wartihog a piece of paper addressed to Stoick.

Gobber the Belch had turned purple in the face. He was still stuck to the wall by his beard with the Kidnapper's axe. A beard was a Hooligan's pride and joy. The redder, the hairier, the tanglier the better, as far as the Hooligans were concerned. It was a terrible insult to lay so much as a *finger* on another Viking's beard –

let alone pin him to the wall with it.

'REVENGE!' bellowed Gobber, trying to pull himself free from the axe but only succeeding in tearing out pieces of his precious beard. 'CHIEF STOICK THE VAST WILL DECLARE A BLOOD FEUD ON THE BOG-BURGLARS WHEN HE HEARS YOU HAVE STOLEN HIS HEIR AND RUINED MY BEARD!'

'These *aren't* Bog-Burglars,' warned Hiccup. 'Bog-Burglars are always women. These aren't women. Look! That one's bosom's just popped. These are *Romans!* Be sure and tell my father that—'

The First Kidnapper clapped a large hand over Hiccup's mouth. But he didn't need to. Gobber wasn't listening to Hiccup anyway. He had gone into a blood-rage just like Stoick ten minutes earlier.

'THE BOG-BURGLARS WILL RUE THE DAY THEY DARED TO MESS WITH THE BEARD OF GOBBER THE BELCH! MAKE NO MISTAKE, I'M GOING TO SEE THE CHIEF ABOUT THIS!'

'You be doings that,' grinned the First Kidnapper, and the Kidnappers left the room, taking Hiccup and Fishlegs with them.

9. WELCOME TO FORT SINISTER

The Kidnappers ran down the hillside with the boys bumping on their backs. They threw them into the bottom of their boat – a small, clearly Roman ship with a very badly made Bog-Burglar flag flying from the mast.

the claws of Rome

The Kidnappers set sail in the opposite direction to the land of the Bog-Burglars.

'Where are we going?' moaned Fishlegs.

'My guess is next stop Fort Sinister,' replied Hiccup.

'Your weedy friend she is right,' sneered the First Kidnapper, removing his false beard. 'You are havings the honour to be kidnapped by the glorious Empire of Rome, and we is takings you to the noble Fortress of Sinister.'

'Yippee,' said Fishlegs gloomily.

'You can be shuttings up now,' said the First Kidnapper, and the boys shut up.

The wind was very strong. Within an hour they had left the safety of Woden's Bathtub and were entering the tricksy currents and needle-sharp rocks of the Mazy Multitudes. This was a bewildering muddle of thousands of small islands some miles south of the Isle of Berk, many with gigantic sea cliffs. Its eerie atmosphere led most Vikings to believe it was haunted.

Huge black mountains with grim scrabbles of rock rose on either side of them. The greasy sea swirled underneath, with every now and then a pointy rock appearing out of nowhere in the mist, so that the Second Kidnapper had to swiftly steer the boat clear.

The closer they got to the Roman Headquarters, the less wildlife there was around them.

Woden's Bathtub had been alive with dragons of all shapes and sizes, screaming and catcalling to each other and skimming across the waves, keeping an eye out for fish. Seals slumbered fatly on the rocks. Birds wheeled in the skies, zooming down on any morsels of fish that went astray during dragonfights.

But as they neared the fort, the seas around them became a desert. Not a bird called, not a fish jumped. The reason for this was clear when they spotted two dead Slitherhawks all tangled up in a gigantic net, hanging from a cliff face.

'And they call US barbarians,' sniffed Fishlegs. Hiccup began to feel a bit sick.

And then his heart skipped a beat. He could hear the sound of dragons screaming, the same noise that they had heard through the mist in Woden's Bathtub… It was a sound that chilled the blood and frayed the nerves, like a sword being sharpened screechily on a stone. He swallowed hard. 'I think we're about to meet the Romans,' he said.

Sure enough, the appalling hullabaloo of

terrified and furious dragons grew louder and louder and louder… then they rounded a corner and there before them, impossibly huge and spooky, stood Fort Sinister.

Their mouths flopped open in astonishment.

Vikings are used to fairly simple living conditions. A Chief just has a larger hut than anybody else. So they had never seen anything the size of Fort Sinister before.

The Island of Sinister was surrounded by enormous black cliffs plunging dizzily down to jagged rocks. On top of these cliffs the Romans had built the biggest fort you could possibly imagine, covering the entire island.

The wind shrieked through its awful towers and great grim cages, the sea seeped through its iron gates and into its terrible dungeons; it was a fort as black and bleak as the rocks it was made out of.

In the middle was the Consul's Palace, a gorgeous villa built around a central courtyard with an ornamental fountain. Next to the Palace was an enormous wooden amphitheatre, and beyond that were the soldiers' barracks.

Countless numbers of dragons were being held in fifty enormous iron cages, with no shelter from the wild wind and bitter cold of the Inner Isles. No wonder they were screaming.

Beyond that were slaves' quarters and kitchens and exercise yards for the horses and training grounds for the gladiators and little temples for the gods and heated swimming baths for the Consul and senior soldiers and stores of ammunition and gigantic equipment for breaking a barricade and field after field of crops.

And this entire, massive area was encircled by

high wooden fences, with watchtowers manned by sentries every hundred metres. Four enormous observation balloons sailed overhead. These balloons were powered by the flaming breath of a dragon kept in a cage just above the basket, and they were manned with more sentries, keeping a sharp eye out for escapees or invaders.

'WOW,' breathed Fishlegs at last. 'No wonder the Romans have conquered most of the world. It's just amazing they haven't conquered US.'

'*Yet,*' said Hiccup grimly. 'And what I'm worrying about is how on earth we're going to GET OUT of here?'

The Kidnappers sailed right up to the wooden entrance gates. These were in themselves impossibly huge, doors larger than some of the sea cliffs on Berk. As they neared, there were cries from the sentries in the watchtowers and the great doors opened to let them in. They sailed through the open gates, right into the heart of the Fortress, and the doors shutting behind them were like the closing of a shark's mouth.

The Second Kidnapper gave the boys a glittering smile as they moored the boat.

'We is welcoming you to Fort Sinister,' he said.

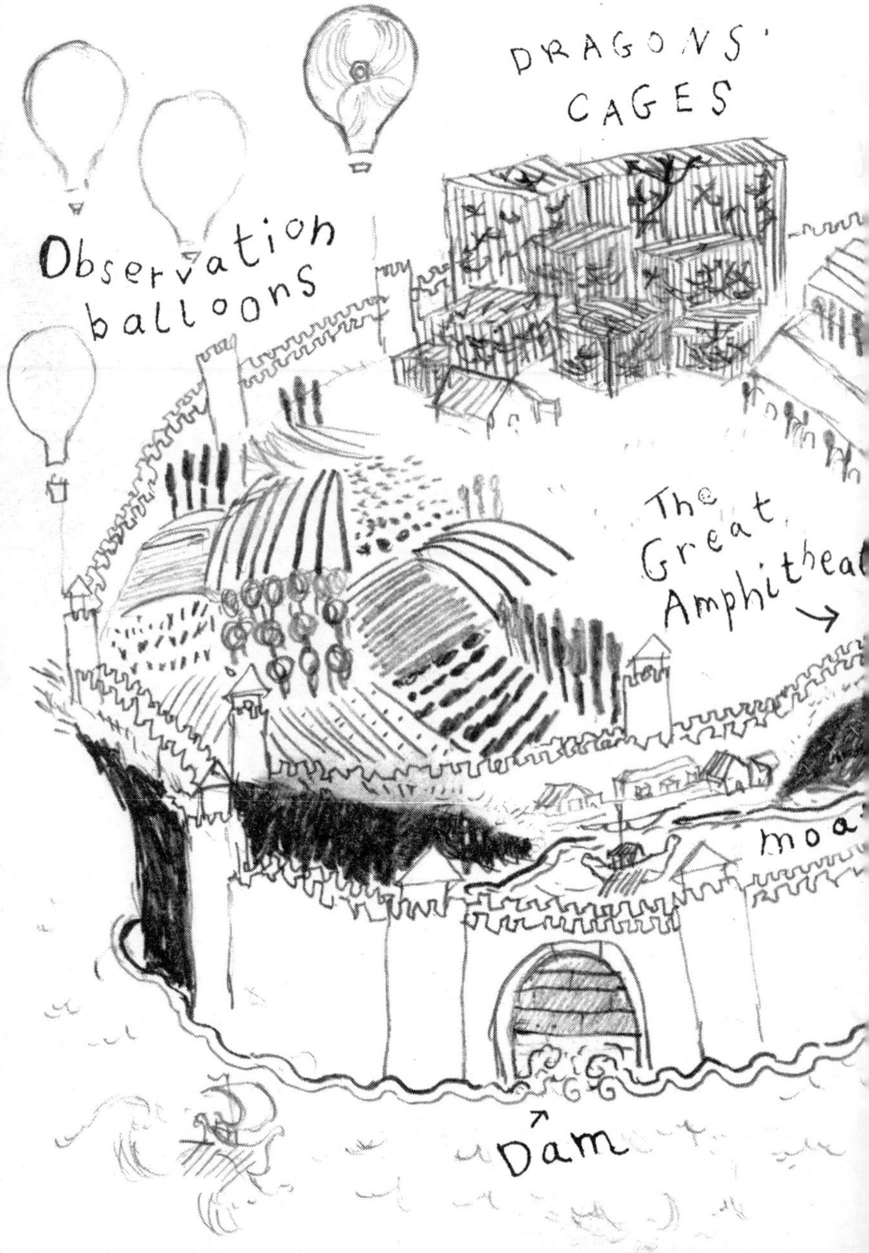

DRAGONS' CAGES

Observation balloons

The Great Amphitheat

moa

Dam

soldiers
barracks

prison
tower

the
Fat Consul's
H.Q.

FORT
SINISTER

10. THE SECRET IDENTITY OF THE THIN PREFECT

The Kidnappers threw the boys over their shoulders again and strode through several large courtyards, busy with soldiers and cooks and horses and people selling things to each other. They walked up some steps and through a door into a brightly lit, gorgeously painted room. This was the Consul's Palace. Tapestries hung from the walls, couches were draped in silken covers, the mosaic floor was warm and toasty underfoot.

The Romans certainly knew how to make themselves comfy.

In one corner of the room, the Fat Consul was having his tonsils tickled with a feather so he could vomit and fit in some more Monstrous Nightmare *Crème Brûlée* for pudding. In another, the Thin Prefect was having his temples massaged. He looked up when they came in and gave an 'Aha!' of evil satisfaction.

At the Prefect's feet lay a particularly large Gronckle, a dragon about two metres high with a spiny ruff around its neck. When they came into the room it heaved its enormous bulk on to its thick muscly legs and an ominous growling began deep in its thick bull neck.

It leaped at the First Kidnapper, who dropped Fishlegs with a scream.

'Stop!' shouted the Thin Prefect in Dragonese. Very *poor* Dragonese, but Dragonese nonetheless. The Gronckle had grabbed the First Kidnapper by the leg in his immense jaws, and the First Kidnapper uselessly drummed his fists on the gigantic creature's great, warty back. The Gronckle had been enjoying itself, gnawing away at the Kidnapper's knee, its great tail lashing from side to side; but at the Thin Prefect's command it reluctantly stopped.

'Think you.' The Thin Prefect had a terrible accent and he kept on getting the words wrong. 'You can hold on to the Kidnapper now.'

The Gronckle didn't move.

'I said "Hold on to him!"' shouted the Thin Prefect crossly.

The Gronckle blinked at him and still didn't move.

'Oh for Thor's sake, you stupid alligator...' swore the Thin Prefect in Norse. From his pocket he got out his half of *How to Speak Dragonese* and started flicking through it, muttering to himself,

'Release, release – what's the word for release?'

'I think you'll find the word is "release", sir?' advised Hiccup politely.

'Thank you,' sneered the Thin Prefect. '"Release",' he said to the Gronckle, who opened its jaws and the Kidnapper dropped, sprawling on to the floor.

'As you can see,' drawled the Thin Prefect, 'I need the other half of your book, Hiccup.'

Hiccup tried not to look as terrified as he felt.

'How do you know my name?' he asked. 'And why are we speaking in Norse, not in Latin?'

The Thin Prefect smiled. 'We have met before, you see, Hiccup, many, many times. Why don't you look a little closer?'

Hiccup looked up into the Thin Prefect's eyes, and he gasped as he finally realised who it was.

The man was bald; completely hairless all over. Even his eyelashes had disappeared. But bald as he was, and dressed in a toga, this was definitely Hiccup's arch-enemy – Alvin the Treacherous, Chief of the Outcast Tribe and the wickedest man in the Inner Isles.

'*So,*' hissed Alvin, 'we meet AGAIN, Hiccup Horrendous Haddock the Third...'

Hiccup and Fishlegs gazed at him in utter astonishment. The last time they had seen Alvin he had been inside the stomach of the Monstrous Strangulator at the bottom of the underground sea-cavern.* How on earth had he got out of THAT tricky situation? And what was he doing posing as a Roman?

'I see you are wondering,' smiled Alvin nastily, 'how I got myself out of THAT tricky situation?'

Fishlegs and Hiccup nodded.

'It's an *interesting* story,' spat Alvin, his eyes hissing with fury. 'I know you'll enjoy it... I cut myself out of the stomach of the dead Monstrous Strangulator with my sword, and then since you had so kindly ABANDONED me without any dragons I couldn't get out of the cavern by the sea...'

'We didn't abandon you!' squeaked Fishlegs. 'We didn't know you were alive! How could we know?'

Alvin ignored him. '... so I had no choice but to go through the Caliban Caves. THREE WHOLE

---

* How to be a Pirate. I would strongly suggest you read this book.

MONTHS it took me, creeping through the darkness, eating little cavern dragons raw, licking the walls for water… and then when I finally emerged into the light on your vile little island and stole a ship back to my own land, what happens? My own people SHUN me – they refuse to have me as their Chief! Because down there in the darkness, in the vile belly of that Strangulator… *something* happened to me…'

Alvin's voice became more and more savage.

'The stomach juices of that infernal creature have made my hair fall out. And whoever has heard of a hairless Viking? I was thrown out of my own Tribe and forced into exile. Luckily, I have some Roman blood on my mother's father's side… and the Empire has use for a clever person like myself. I told them I had thought of a way they could conquer the Vikings by turning the Tribes against each other.'

'TRAITOR!' yelled Fishlegs.

'Exactly,' smiled Alvin. 'And I also have my own plans for a… DRAGON ARMY.' Alvin drew his right arm out of his toga for the first time. An arm that ended not in a hand but in a huge curved HOOK made out of the most brilliant gold.

'I made this hook,' he said casually, 'out of a

Alvin the Treacherous

single cup of that Treasure. It was the only thing I could carry through the Caliban Caves. But I want the rest of it – I need the rest of it...

'With a DRAGON ARMY I can get the Treasure,' continued Alvin. 'The dragons can swim down and bring it up for me. But you know what I need first, Hiccup...'

Alvin drew the point of his hook right against Hiccup's chest. 'I need the other half of that book of yours, *How to Speak Dragonese*. I need that book to command the dragons in my Dragon Army. Where is your half of the book, Hiccup? If you tell me I will let

you and your fishlegged friend live. Otherwise I'm afraid I'm going to have to kill you both RIGHT NOW...'

'Tell me what you've done with Toothless first,' said Hiccup.

'Oh, Toothless is very safe,' grinned Alvin. 'He's locked up in one of my dungeons.'

Hiccup gave a sigh of relief. At least he wasn't dead.

'Give me the book now,' commanded Alvin.

'If I give it to you, will you promise you won't kill us?' asked Hiccup.

'I promise,' smiled Alvin.

Hiccup felt into his pocket and handed Alvin his damp and tattered half of *How to Speak Dragonese*. He knew Alvin would find it at some point anyway.

'Thank you,' sneered Alvin. He unscrewed the hook from the end of his arm and replaced it with his famous sword, the Stormblade.

'Uh-oh,' said Hiccup.

The Fat Consul had finally polished off a large helping of roasted baby Puff Nadders in garlicky Dreamserpent sauce, and he started to take an interest in what was going on.

ELEVENSES MENU

for His Most Noble Fatness The Fat Consul

HORS D'OEUVRES

Roasted baby Puff Nadders in garlicky
Dreamserpent sauce

Larks tongue soup with crunchy
nanodragon heads on the side

ENTRÉES

Whole roast ox marinated in pickled
Slitherhawk and shark's eyeballs

Double Reptoburger with extra cheese
and picallilli penguins

Live Frog-and-Dormouse soufflées in
Common or Garden sauce

PAUSE FOR A VOMIT

LES DESSERTS

Monstrous Nightmare Crème Brulee with
smoked haddock and chocolate mousse

Sticky toffee Nadder and whelk pudding

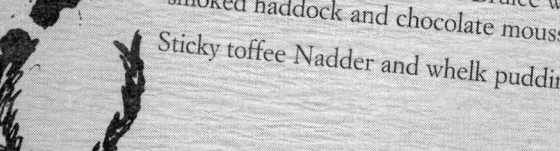

'Who have you got over there, Prefect?' he drawled, wiping the cream from the third of his chins. Hiccup noticed that he wasn't looking too well. He was covered from head to toe in nasty red bites, and every now and then he reached out a fat arm to scratch his gigantic blubbery behind.

'This,' said Alvin grimly, 'is the Heir to the Hairy Hooligans.'

'The extraordinarily powerful warrior you were telling me about?' asked the Fat Consul. He looked at Hiccup in astonishment.

'But he's so very, very small!'

'Size isn't everything,' replied Alvin the Treacherous.

'What are you going to do with him then, Prefect?' asked the Fat Consul.

'I'm going to kill him,' said Alvin, giving the Stormblade a nasty swish.

'You promised you wouldn't!' protested Hiccup.

'Tsk, tsk,' tutted Alvin, 'haven't you learned by now that a Treacherous never keeps his promise?'

'Hang on a second, my dear Prefect,' drawled the Fat Consul. 'It seems a waste to kill him now. Let him live until Saturn's day Saturday – I would like to see this extraordinary warrior in action in the gladiatorial arena…'

'That's not a good idea, Consul,' said Alvin. 'This boy may not look much, but I assure you I have seen him in action and he could ruin all our plans. We must kill him NOW while we have the chance.'

'Who gives the orders round here?' asked the Fat Consul.

'I d—' Alvin recollected himself just in time. 'I mean, *you* do, of course, Consul,' Alvin bowed fawingly at him, 'but—'

'No arguing, please, Prefect,' ordered the Consul.

'At least let me kill the one who looks like a haddock,' pleaded Alvin the Treacherous.

'Fishlegs is a BERSERK*, you know, Consul,' said Hiccup hurriedly. 'I'm sure he'd put on a very exciting fighting display as a gladiator.'

'*Really?*' exclaimed the Fat Consul. 'This is proving a very interesting morning. I've never

---

* You know the expression 'going berserk'? Well, Berserks were Vikings who went crazy on the battlefield. Good men to have on your side. Not so good when they were on the *other* side, though…

met a Berserk before. He should be most amusing at the Games. The one with the face like a fish lives too, I'm afraid, Prefect.'

'But sir—'

The Fat Consul waved away Alvin's objections with one fat hand.

'Put the prisoners in the dungeon with the Bog-Burglar Heir!'

Alvin fought to control his temper. He smiled at the Consul through very gritted teeth. 'Of course you know best, sir,' he said. 'But don't blame me if it all goes wrong...'

Alvin turned to the Gronckle. **'Sit on me!'** he ordered in his extremely poor Dragonese, **'and put me in the toilet with the other Heirs!'**

The Gronckle promptly sat on Alvin. The First Kidnapper had to prod the dragon very hard with the handle of his sword to get the Gronckle off before he squashed Alvin entirely. When he finally emerged from underneath the creature's bottom, Alvin was hopping mad.

'No, no, no!' he shrieked, and then tried to put together the two halves of *How to Speak Dragonese*, muttering swearwords under his breath as he looked for the right page. 'Ah, here it is!' he said with satisfaction. 'Pick my nose and put me in the toilet with the Bog-Burglar Heir!'

The Second Kidnapper had to lash out furiously with his sword-handle to prevent the Gronckle from picking Alvin's nose with its gigantic talons. And then the creature picked Alvin up and started trying to stuff him in the Fat Consul's gigantic toilet.

Alvin in the toilet

Yucky!

131

'Carry on!' shrieked Alvin.

'Can *I* help?' asked Hiccup. He talked to the Gronckle directly. 'I think what the Prefect is TRYING to say is, pick US up and put US in the Tower with the Bog-Burglar Heir...'

The Gronckle picked up Hiccup and Fishlegs by the scruffs of their necks as if they were two kittens.

'At least,' pleaded Hiccup to Alvin as he swung from the Gronckle's jaws, 'won't you do a good thing for once in your life and set Toothless free? You don't need him and he's never done anything to *you*...'

Alvin tried to look dignified as he climbed out of the toilet.

Which was tricky.

'That isn't true,' he said. 'That dragon once did a poo in my helmet. A Treacherous Never Forgives. He can stay in that dungeon and rot for all I care... Actually, I've just had a better idea – he can join you in the arena on Saturn's day Saturday and you can all die a horrible death together...' Alvin gave a gruesome smirk and waved his hand at the Gronckle.

'Take them away,' he ordered, for once getting the Dragonese right, and the Gronckle trotted off to the Tower with the boys in his mouth, followed by the First Kidnapper. The huge animal clattered up the wooden steps and stopped outside a large door. This was the door to the prison where Alvin was keeping the other Heir. The First Kidnapper opened it with a large key that was hanging from his belt.

'Welcomes to your home for three weeks, please,' he smirked unpleasantly. 'Do much swordfightings… Roman gladiators are very, very good, me thinkings…'

'At least we'll meet the heir to the Bog-Burglars,' said Hiccup to Fishlegs. 'Maybe this whole mess is a chance to meet her and make some sort of peace between the Hooligans and the Bog-Burglars…'

11. THE BOG-BURGLAR HEIR

The Gronckle trotted into the room. It was a large, bare space with a table and a few chairs and some straw in the corner that served for beds. The windows were barred. The boys were clearly not going to have the same luxuries the Romans gave themselves. The Gronckle dropped Fishlegs and Hiccup on the floor and backed out of the room.

'Making yourselves at home,' sneered the First Kidnapper, and the door clanged shut.

Standing in the middle of the room was a small girl with wild blonde hair and a ferocious expression.

The girl drew her sword with a flourish.

'Who are *you*? What are your names?' she demanded fiercely. 'Who sent you? Where do you come from?'

'My name is Hiccup,' stammered Hiccup. 'And this is Fishlegs – we're Hooligans…'

'I don't believe you!' yelled the little girl. 'You're Roman spies! Draw your swords and FIGHT like *men*, you Latin low lives!'

The boys looked at the furious little girl in amazement.

Fishlegs began to laugh.

Camicazi

He wasn't laughing two seconds later when the little girl cut the cord of his trousers and they fell down around his ankles.

'Hey!' objected Fishlegs, indignantly hauling them up again. 'Watch what you're doing with that sword!'

In reply the little girl hoisted the sword over her head and ran towards Hiccup shouting the Bog-Burglar War Cry, which sounds like a very rude word shouted at the top of the lungs. Hiccup drew his sword just in time to parry her lunge, and they began to fight.

Last year, Hiccup had found out that he was left-handed. Since then, he had discovered he had a gift for sword-fighting. It was the only thing on the Pirate Training Programme he was truly good at. He could beat even Oikish and Dogsbreath quite easily, and was having extra lessons with Gormless the Grim, the best sword-fighter in the Hooligan Tribe.

But this little girl was just as good at sword-fighting as Hiccup. Her arm moved so quickly you could hardly see it. She turned cartwheels between moves. And she TALKED constantly throughout, which made it difficult to concentrate.

'FIGHT, you nano-eating, locust-baking, toga-wearing, Jupiter-worshipper! Ooooh you're actually quite *good* at this – for a *boy* – I've been getting SO bored, you have no idea...'

'Can't we just have a quiet talk about this?' asked Hiccup breathlessly. 'There really is no need for us to be fighting...'

But the little girl took absolutely no notice of him and carried on talking.

'I see you know the *Grimbeard's Grapple*, and the *Flashcut Lunge*, and the *Deathwatch Parry*, and the—'

'Will you STOP!' panted Hiccup, frantically parrying all of these moves, and getting his sleeve cut off in the process. 'My name really *is* Hiccup... I really *am* a Hooligan...'

'I don't believe you,' said the little girl. 'You're a Roman SPY! Admit it, or I will UNZIP you from your BREADBASKET to your OYSTERGOBBLER! *Oooooooh* your defence is a bit WEAK, you know, you should really *work* on that... otherwise, a person could just *nip* through – and...'

She made a perfectly executed lunge which Hiccup parried at the last minute but which cut off his second sleeve.

'Whoops!' crowed the little girl joyfully. 'There goes the *other* one!'

'I – AM – NOT – A – ROMAN...' gasped Hiccup, his back against the wall.

'Well, a Hooligan isn't much better,' said the little girl, pausing for a second and then carrying on. 'My mother says the only good Hooligan is a dead Hooligan.'

'That's funny,' panted Hiccup, 'because *my father* says that the only good Bog-Burglar is a dead Bog-Burglar – and the *really* amusing thing is, unless we join together, in about two weeks' time, we are

both going to be VERY GOOD, and VERY DEAD.'

'Oh BOTHER,' sighed the girl, stopping at last. Now that she wasn't moving around so much, Hiccup could see that she really was quite a small girl, at least a head shorter than he was. 'I was really looking *forward* to spilling some blood.'

She grinned at Hiccup. 'You're not a *bad* swordfighter, actually, for a boy, of course…'

'Thanks,' said Hiccup, still trying to catch his breath.

The little girl stuck out her hand for a handshake. 'My name's CAMICAZI, the Heir to the Bog-Burglars. Nice to meet you. What are *you* doing here, anyway?'

'We got kidnapped just like you,' replied Hiccup. 'And we're also looking for a dragon that I've lost. He's about so high, green eyes, a Common-or-Garden…'

'Oh, yes,' said Camicazi. 'The soldier who brings the food *told* me about HIM. He bit the Prefect on the nose when they brought him in!'

'Good old Toothless,' said Hiccup.

'The Prefect really doesn't like HIM,' said Camicazi.

'Yes I know,' said Hiccup. 'Toothless once did a poo in his helmet, and a Treacherous never forgives.'

'They've put him in Level Seven, Top Security.'

'Oh poor, *poor* Toothless,' said Hiccup. 'I can't bear to think of him being trapped. He hates small spaces – he can't even go down rabbit holes, despite rabbit being his favourite food; he stays at the entrance shrieking his head off—'

But at that very moment the door to the prison cell opened again. It was a stout soldier carrying a small green ball in one hand.

'I've got a present for Hiccup Horrendous Haddock the Third from the Prefect,' leered the soldier.

He threw the ball roughly at Hiccup and it struck him heavily in the stomach, winding him severely. The little ball unrolled itself with a furious 'D-d-d-do you m-m-mind?' and with a sudden burst of happiness Hiccup realised who it was.

'Toothless!' he exclaimed joyfully, once he had got his breath back. 'TOOTHLESS!'

He bent down to pick up his dragon. The poor little animal had lost so much weight he was all skin and bones. Hiccup could feel his ribs sticking out, and his tail had gone all floppy and lost its pointy fork which is what happens if a dragon is imprisoned or deeply unhappy.

For a moment Toothless pretended that he didn't care – 'Y-y-yucky – put me down!' – and then he put his little dragon arms around Hiccup's neck and hung on for dear life, whispering in Hiccup's ear, so that only he could hear, over and over again 'Th-th-thank you... thank you... T-T-Toothless would have died if he spent one more hour in that h-h-horrible place... TH-TH-THANK YOU...'

12. THE MASTER-ESCAPER

It may not sound like much, but one of the first facts you learn about dragons is that they are hardly *ever* grateful. This was the first time in Toothless's life he had thanked Hiccup for anything.

He soon recovered himself, and to make up for this moment of weakness he gave Hiccup an embarrassed nip on the ear.

He then became thoroughly over-excited and twirled himself around Hiccup's neck three times, before diving down Hiccup's shirt and running all over his chest and round his back and under his armpits, which made Hiccup laugh a lot, because the light pattering of a dragon's feet and the swirl of its tail is almost unbearably ticklish.

'Stop it!' shouted Hiccup, in between gasps of laughter. Toothless emerged from the shirt and scurried on to Hiccup's head, his little green paws making Hiccup's hair stand up on end even more than it did already. Sitting high up on Hiccup's forehead, Toothless puffed out his chest and crowed three joyful 'Cock-a-Doodle-Doos' of triumph.

Camicazi watched all this with interest,

particularly the strange pops and whistles that Hiccup made with his mouth when talking back to Toothless in Dragonese.

'Oh, I've heard about you,' she said. 'You're the geek who talks to dragons…'

'Talking to dragons is not geeky,' said Hiccup crossly. 'Dragonwhispering is a very ancient and rare skill.'

'OK,' said Fishlegs. 'So if we've rescued *Toothless*, I have just one question – who's going to rescue US?'

'We're going to rescue OURSELVES, of course!' cried Camicazi, drawing her sword again. 'We ESCAPE or we DIE!' she shouted with a mad gleam in her eye. 'As it *happens*, I am the master escaper, this isn't the first time I've been kidnapped, you know.'

'The MASTER ESCAPER,' snorted Fishlegs, 'You Bog-Burglars are very pleased with yourselves. Who's kidnapped you before?'

'Oh… other Viking Tribes, mostly,' replied

Camicazi carelessly. She hummed a little tune and happily swung her sword around her head.

'The Meatheads... the Visithugs... us Bog-Burglars are always quarrelling with EVERYBODY... we have anger issues... anyway, I escaped from the Visithugs, no problem...'

'*No problem?*' said Fishlegs. The Visithugs were supposed to be TOUGH.

'I think you'll have a problem escaping from a Roman Fortress,' said Hiccup, stroking Toothless who was beginning to purr. 'Roman Fortresses are built to be impossible to get into and impossible to get out of. Have you noticed the four perimeter fences? The four observation balloons? The guards at every watchtower? Not to mention the bars on this cell and the locked door. I don't think you've got a hope of escaping.'

Camicazi smiled confidently. 'Nothing is beyond the powers of a master escaper,' she assured them. 'You can't keep a Bog-Burglar under lock and key. No prisons can hold us – we're as wriggly as eels...'

'So why are you still here then if you're such a great escaper?' said Fishlegs.

'I suggest that we wait for my father to send a War Party to rescue us,' said Hiccup.

'He didn't send a War Party to rescue Toothless,' Fishlegs pointed out.

'Yes but I *nearly* persuaded him to,' replied Hiccup eagerly. 'I think I really got through to him… And I am his SON after all, and not just a dragon…'

Toothless gave him a reproachful bite.

'He'll come, I know he will,' said Hiccup. 'I think I'll just sit here and wait for him.' And Hiccup sat down on a stool by the barred window that looked out over the sea in the direction of Berk. It was raining, a dull never-ending sort of rain that would have you soaking wet in two seconds if you went out in it. 'He will come, I'm telling you.'

But Hiccup was anxious. His father had been so disappointed with Hiccup's report. Maybe his father thought that Snotlout, who always got 10 out of 10 in everything, would make a better Heir than Hiccup… Maybe his father was relieved Hiccup had gone…. Maybe, just maybe, his father wasn't coming at all…

13. BACK ON BERK

Back on Berk, Stoick the Vast sat in front of the table in his Chiefly Hut with his head in his hands.

'A Chief feels no pain…' he was saying to himself over and over again. 'A Chief feels no fear… A Chief is above mere weak personal feelings…'

But oddly enough this didn't seem to make him feel any better.

'There will be other sons…' he said to himself. And the wind howling across the ocean and through the wet bracken and blowing open the doors in a flurry of rain seemed to call back to him…

'… but not like Hiccup.'

What kind of a Chief am I? he thought to himself wretchedly. *Grimbeard the Ghastly would never have hesitated like this! Grimbeard the Ghastly would know it was the Bog-Burglars' fault yet again. He'd have been over there bashing those Bog-Burglars all the way to Valhalla by now…*

But then he caught sight of the Roman helmet, and doubts started to creep in.

Could it possibly be that Hiccup was right and the Romans had found their way into the Inner Isles

149

and were trying to make trouble?

Sighing, he picked up the piece of paper sitting on the table in front of him. On it he had written:

Plan A: Sale to the land of the Bog-Burglars and starte bashing everybody.

He picked up the quill, dipped it in the ink and wrote:

Plan B: Send a War Partty to look for A Romman Forte.

But which was the right thing to do?
Being a Chief was a lonely business.

14. CAMICAZI'S ESCAPE PLANS

For the next week Hiccup sat by the barred window looking out for his father's War Party.

Toothless came and sat on Hiccup's head. This was a familiar ritual to both of them, as it was Toothless's usual seat when Hiccup was dragonwatching at the Wild Dragon Cliff. Hiccup would draw and write in his Dragonese book, while Toothless perched on his head, one eye shut, the other half open, watching out for careless rabbits or small mice that he could catch. They could sit there for hours in

happy, companionable silence.

Now they sat looking out the window, searching, searching, for the boats that were not there.

They were being held in a barred tower room high in the air. The one good thing about being held prisoner was that they didn't have to go outside.

Because outside it was raining. Not your ordinary, average kind of spitty little rain, but rain such as you only really get in the Barbaric Archipelago, one

of the wettest places on this good green earth. For the whole week it rained as if the sky above was one big endless bucket of water, pouring down without stopping on the poor souls beneath.

The Romans are excellent travellers, but they are not used to this kind of weather. Nobody is. Hiccup watched with interest from his tower window high above as the soldiers' training grounds turned into one big puddly mess of black mud. The Consul's heated swimming baths overflowed into the horses' exercise yards. The kitchens were knee deep in water. Even the Tower itself seemed to sink a few centimetres as its foundations softened and oozed.

The one good thing about the rain was that it silenced the screeching dragons being held prisoner in the giant cages down below. Dragons tend to sleep through rain. Their skin is waterproof, so they put up their wings like umbrellas, and sleep underneath them.

Inside the Tower room, although it was bare, it was at least dry. The young Vikings were allowed to keep their swords and shields to practise for their appearance in the arena on Saturn's day Saturday.

A soldier brought them food every day. There was lots of it, although it was all a bit too rich for Hiccup's liking. Pig stuffed with dormice stuffed with baby frogs carbonara and oysters fried in cream is a bit of an acquired taste. They all refused to eat it when it was fried dragon pie or Common-or-Gardens in batter.

Toothless hardly ate at all. Hiccup tried to persuade him but Toothless put his nose up.

'Roman f-f-food YUCKY,' he said. 'Too much g-g-garlic. Want some good f-f-fish. Want mackerel.'

Camicazi carried on with her escape plans. They were all completely crazy.

For the first one she persuaded Hiccup and Fishlegs to help her knit their waistcoats into two ropes and she attached one end of a rope to a fish head and the other to one of the bars in the window. She then spent three nights in a row throwing the fish head out the window, hoping for a passing dragon to catch it. Finally her patience was rewarded when it

was snapped up by a hungry Gronckle who flew off with it, the rope pulling out the bar in the window before it snapped.

Camicazi squirmed out the window and down the rope, which dangled twenty metres above the ground. She held on for as long as she could, but eventually had to let go, and landed on a fat soldier playing dice under an umbrella with a dozen fellow soldiers below.

They were then moved to another, supposedly more secure, cell on the ground floor.

Camicazi wasn't about to give up with this little setback, though. She spent four days tunnelling her way out of their new prison with Hiccup's helmet. Unfortunately the tunnel came out right slap bang in the middle of the Consul's bathroom. A naked Fat Consul screeched for reinforcements and they were moved back to the Tower room again, where the window had been repaired.

Her third plan was the craziest of all.

She ambushed the soldier who brought them their food every day, knocking him out with his own food tray.

She was planning to wear his clothes to pass herself off as a soldier.

'It'll never work,' said Hiccup. 'You'll get caught. You're a girl for starters. And you're only four foot high. There are no four-foot-high soldiers. They don't let them in the army.'

'Oh, you're always bringing up PROBLEMS,' grumbled Camicazi, putting on the soldier's helmet, which was so big she could hardly see out of it.

'And let's face it, they're going to be really cross you knocked out one of their men,' Hiccup pointed out, looking at the soldier slumbering peacefully in his Roman underwear on the floor.

'Why don't YOU face it?' snapped Camicazi. 'Look at you, staring out the window all day long. Your father is NEVER GOING TO COME...'

Hiccup flinched.

'He'll come,' he said defiantly.

Camicazi had to turn up the sleeves of the soldier's shirt four times. The tunic trailed some way along the ground behind her. She looked like a very small military person in a wedding dress.

'Ze great CAMICAZI will be back home, guys, while *you* are facing those gladiators on Saturn's day Saturday...'

She took three steps and fell flat on her face.

The boys tried very hard not to laugh.

With great dignity Camicazi got back on to her

feet again. She picked up the front of the tunic like she really was a bride. 'You can't keep a Bog-Burglar under lock and key,' she said, taking the keys from the tunic pocket and unlocking the cell door. With a final bustle of skirts she was gone.

Hiccup looked out the window again.

'He'll come...' said Hiccup. The rain was being blown through the window at such a rate that he had been driven from his usual post. But now he peered through the bars, seeking, seeking, for the sails that were not there. There was only rain and more rain, pouring down relentlessly on the ocean, drumming on the rocks, sogging up the heather, and filling the

pockets of the poor sentries as they stood, sandals full of mud, dreaming of Roman sunshine.

The wind shrieked across the ocean, up over the grim black cliffs, and through the Roman courtyards of the fort. And as it came through Hiccup's barred window, blowing in great drenching streams of water, it seemed to be answering…

'… but he's late…'

Camicazi didn't return that night. Hiccup and Fishlegs wondered with amazement if she really *had* escaped this time. But the soldier who brought their food that evening very grumpily told them she had been caught within two seconds of leaving the Tower and put into solitary confinement for three days.

'And serve her right, the little barbarian,' said the soldier, rubbing the lump on his head.

'Three days!' said Fishlegs excitedly. 'At least we'll have some peace and quiet around here.'

'...dreaming of Roman sunshine...'

'Camicazi's all right really,' said Hiccup.

'Mmmm,' said Fishlegs, unconvinced. 'But she's very pleased with herself and she never stops talking. I'm looking forward to a nice, quiet night.'

15. THE COMING OF THE SHARKWORMS

As the long night wore on, something strange and frightening was happening in the seas around Fort Sinister.

The rain poured down without stopping, and for several days the heated swimming baths of the Fat Consul had been overflowing, sending a stream of hot water pouring down the hillside and into the ocean.

And this warm current was attracting some unwelcome visitors… SHARKWORMS.

From far and wide the Sharkworms came. Terrible creatures half out of nightmares, but only too true I'm afraid, propelled not only by the tremendous force of a shark-like tail, but also by thick, muscly alligator legs that poured through the water, sending them forward at extraordinary speeds.

They were swimming towards the Roman Fortress, not just in ones and twos but in tens of thousands, and when the sun came up on the morning before Saturn's day Saturday there was a boiling mass of black fins with jagged edges, circling like vultures around the island of Fort Sinister.

It was as if they were waiting for something. Sharkworms are ancient animals and their brains were formed in who knows what dark and terrible furnace. They knew not *why* they waited, only that they smelled warm water, and blood-yet-to-be-spilled, and guts-in-the-offing and trouble-about-to-happen.

And so they waited, patiently and greedily, waiting and waiting and waiting for some awful event to unfold in the future that would bring them their supper.

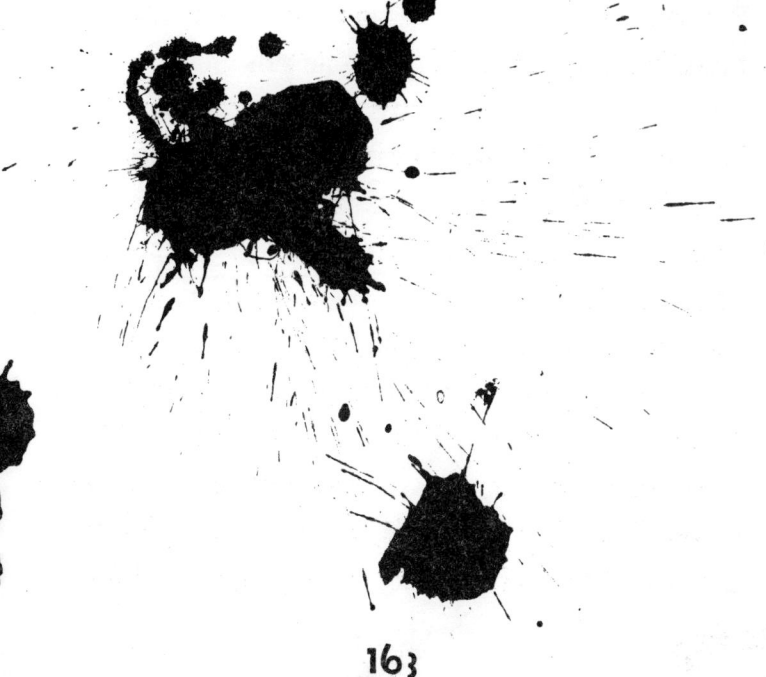

16. THE CUNNING BUT DESPERATE PLAN

Camicazi returned the day before Saturn's day Saturday.

She was not as cheerful as usual. She drooped around the cell, sighing. Even Fishlegs was worried. Camicazi came and sat next to Hiccup beside the barred window.

'Maybe,' she said sadly, 'maybe you *can* keep a Bog-Burglar under lock and key. I don't understand it. I'm the MASTER ESCAPER – no prison can hold me…'

'The Romans make good prisons,' replied Hiccup.

'The only *good* Roman is a *dead* Roman,' said Camicazi.

Hiccup sighed. 'That isn't true. I'm sure there are *loads* of good Romans. But all the good Romans are probably quietly minding their own business back in Rome. Anyway, Alvin isn't a Roman, he's a Viking just like us.'

'Your father really ISN'T going to send a War

Party, you know Hiccup,' said Camicazi gently.

Hiccup looked out the window. Camicazi was right. HIS FATHER WASN'T COMING. Maybe he thought that Hiccup wasn't worth it…

'OK,' said Hiccup, trying to keep them from despairing. 'I think it's time we made another plan.'

'*I* know what we do!' cried Camicazi, drawing her sword with her old swagger back again. 'We practise our sword-fighting! We die, *yes* – but we die in STYLE!'

'No,' said Hiccup.

'But you're a great sword-fighter – for a *boy*, of course…' said Camicazi, disappointed.

'I only sword-fight when there's a point to it,' said Hiccup. 'No, *this* is the plan. I have this dragon called Ziggerastica who owes me a favour…'

'OOOooh, Ziggerastica – he sounds scary,' said Camicazi. 'Do you think he can help us?'

'I don't know,' Hiccup admitted.

Hiccup felt a bit silly shouting to someone who wasn't in the room, but he did so nonetheless, calling 'ZIGGERASTICA!' three times at the top of his voice.

'How is this dragon going to get IN here, when

we can't get OUT?' asked Camicazi.

'You'll see,' said Hiccup.

Nothing happened for about three hours. Hiccup wasn't really expecting this plan to work, in his heart of hearts – he was just trying to cheer Camicazi up. But then there was a faint rustling noise, and the tiny black and red dragon squeezed through the double bars and fluttered around the room.

'Don't tell me,' said Camicazi, '*please* don't tell me that THIS is the dragon who owes you the favour…'

'Yup,' said Hiccup in astonishment. 'That's definitely him.

How *amazing* that he came when I called!'

'This dragon,' said Fishlegs, 'is even smaller than Toothless – that's *really* going to help us, isn't it? The entire Roman Army is going to be shivering in its shoes when it sets eyes on a dragon the size of a bumblebee. How can a dragon not much larger than a beetle help us fight a whole Roman Legion?'

'What were you expecting?' asked Hiccup. 'A Seadragonus Giganticus Maximus? Hang on, Toothless… what are you doing?'

Toothless was stalking Ziggerastica like a cat following a mouse.

'Toothless, STOP!' yelled Hiccup. 'You mustn't eat him, he's our only chance of getting out of here alive!'

But Toothless hadn't had the pleasure of hunting for a couple of weeks now. He chased a shrieking Ziggerastica all around the room until he finally trapped him in a corner of the ceiling and closed his jaws around him.

Toothless hovered just out of reach, one cheek bulging, and Ziggerastica's furiously swinging tail trailing out of his mouth.

'SPIT HIM OUT!' howled Hiccup, frantically jumping up and trying to grab Toothless by the tail. 'I mean it, Toothless, this is not a game – our lives depend on that nanodragon!'

Toothless shot him a naughty look and dodged to the other corner of the room.

The others joined in the chase, leaping after Toothless as he swooped from one side of the ceiling to the other, squealing with delight.

Camicazi climbed on to Fishlegs's shoulders, while Hiccup got on a chair and tried to sweep Toothless in her direction with a broom.

Unfortunately, Hiccup missed, and the brush

cannoned into Camicazi and Fishlegs, who then
knocked over the chair Hiccup was standing on and
they all landed in a heap on the floor.

Toothless somersaulted across the ceiling in his
glee. He laughed so hard he nearly dropped
Ziggerastica. He hadn't had so much fun in ages.

'OK,' said Hiccup under his breath to the
other two, 'I've got a new tactic here…

'We don't have time for this nonsense,' Hiccup said loudly. 'Just ignore Toothless and everybody gather round me while I tell you our plan...'

'Oh, I get it,' said Fishlegs.

Fishlegs and Camicazi got into a huddle around Hiccup who started whispering loudly.

Toothless remained on the ceiling, making rude raspberry noises.

Nobody paid him any attention.

Eventually Toothless's curiosity got the better of him, and he flapped down to see if he could hear what was being said – and Camicazi leaped out of the huddle and grabbed him.

'HA!' said Hiccup triumphantly, looking sternly down on the struggling little dragon. 'Now, Toothless, DROP IT.'

Toothless crossed his eyes and made a gulping noise with his throat as if he was swallowing...

'AAAAAAARGH!' screamed Hiccup.

Toothless spat Ziggerastica on to the floor.

'Only j-j-joking,' he said.

Ziggerastica was FURIOUS.

Hiccup put him carefully on the table and for five minutes he refused to say anything at all, concentrating on shaking out his wings and removing Toothless's saliva.

'I am SO sorry about Toothless, Your Highness,' said Hiccup, thinking that a little flattery might be necessary.

Ziggerastica's voice was icy. 'If I didn't owe you a favour, O-Boy-With-Legs-Like-a-Heron,' he spat, 'that dragon would be history...'

Toothless laughed scornfully. 'What you g-g-gonna do, tough guy? T-t-tickle Toothless to d-d-death?'

'Shut up, Toothless,' said Hiccup. 'Thank you for coming, Ziggerastica. And for looking so very, VERY handsome as well, if I may say so...You have such kingly legs...'

Ziggerastica looked

slightly less cross. He admired his own royal knees with approval.

'And your wings! The finest I have ever seen! I'll explain what I would like Your Highness to do...'

Hiccup told the nanodragon his cunning but truly desperate plan.

The nanodragon was silent for a moment.

'That,' he said at last, 'is a truly terrible plan.'

'T-t-told you,' said Toothless. 'H-h-hiccup's plans are always terrible...'

'You're still alive, aren't you?' retorted Hiccup.

'Also,' said the nanodragon, 'that is actually two favours, and I have offered you only one.'

'Think how cross the Fat Consul will be...' pleaded Hiccup.

The nanodragon thought about that. He shook out his black and red spotty wings, and Hiccup began to see the suggestion of a smile on his tiny face.

'OK,' said Ziggerastica, 'I'll do it. But don't blame me if it fails... By the way, O-Boy-With-a-Nose-Like-a-Small-Potato, your friends are even uglier than you are! Where did you find these people? Never in my life have I seen anybody who looks so much like a lemon sole...' He pointed rudely at Fishlegs with one wing.

And with that the little nanodragon gave a self-

important wriggle of
his behind and flew
out the window.

'Did he agree
to carry out your
plan?' asked
Camicazi.

Hiccup
nodded, trying to
look confident to
keep everybody's
hopes up.

'The thing is,' he
said, 'I don't think in this
kind of weather they'll be able to hold those Games
tomorrow anyway. I've seen the arena from the
window, and it's knee-deep in water – the ground is
far too wet and slippy for gladiatorial combat. With
any luck the rain will make them cancel the whole
thing.'

17. THE CIRCUS ON SATURN'S DAY SATURDAY

The next day was Saturn's day Saturday. For the first time in a week the wind dropped and the clouds cleared. It was a glorious day for a celebration, the sky a bright blue with not a breath of rain. From about ten o'clock in the morning Hiccup watched the stadium being prepared for the circus. The stands were hung with Roman flags. Tents and cushions were laid out in the Consul's seating area. Metal nets were set up across the top and insides of the amphitheatre to prevent the performing dragons from escaping or attacking the audience.

The stands of the amphitheatre began to fill up with spectators, anxious to get a good view. They were mostly soldiers, cooks and carpenters, given the day off for the national holiday. They could buy food and wine within the amphitheatre to while away the hours, so, by early afternoon, when the performances began, the atmosphere was very lively, everybody singing songs and even dancing on the seats.

At two o'clock exactly the trumpeters came out

on to the Consul's Pavilion, the luxury covered area which was draped with Roman flags and Imperial Standards. They blew an impressive fanfare, and everyone stood up and fell silent as the Consul's party entered the stadium. The Fat Consul came first,

The Great Amphitheatre

with wire netting set over the arena ↓

← water flooding in

waddling very slowly with a slave at each elbow and one to carry his stomach. He had to stop every couple of steps to catch his breath.

He wasn't looking too good. The Fat Consul was covered from head to toe in ugly red rashes and eczema weals. Once the slaves had got him seated, they took it in turns to scratch different parts of his body with an instrument like a large fork, and this seemed to give him some relief, but judging from his restless wriggling and scratching he was still in considerable discomfort.

He was eating a light snack of double reptoburger with tomato-and-dormouse relish and popdragons on the side.

Alvin the Treacherous sat beside him in the Pavilion. In time to another trumpet fanfare two slaves brought in the Ceremonial Shield of the Legion, gorgeously decorated with a golden eagle carrying a fish. Alvin the Treacherous banged the Ceremonial Shield three times with his hook.

'I officially declare these Saturn's day Saturday Games OPEN,' shouted Alvin the Treacherous. 'Friends and fellow Romans...Watch our Circus and marvel at the glory of the Roman

Empire! Your entertainment this afternoon is called THE SURVIVAL OF THE FITTEST...'

The audience clapped wildly.

Three hundred beautiful doves, dyed every colour of the rainbow, were released into the arena. The doves fluttered through the stadium, cooing to each other.

Suddenly, the barred gates opened and the coos of the doves turned to cries of alarm. To the cheers and catcalls of the audience, fifty little Sidewinder dragons came slithering through the dust into the arena, their greengage eyes glistening greedily.

The Sidewinders were not large but they were vicious pack hunters. They were also chameleons. Every one of them was exactly the colour of the dust they were lying in.

The doves desperately threw themselves against the metal nets covering the amphitheatre but there was no escape for them.

The Sidewinders crept into the air like an army of cats stalking sparrows. As they rose up they gradually turned as pale blue as the sky above them, and the doves flew desperately hither and thither in confusion, until the leader of the Sidewinders gave the signal to attack.

Less than sixty seconds later the air was filled with blood and multi-coloured feathers and there was not a dove left alive in that stadium.

The Sidewinders celebrated by turning the colour of the dove they had just eaten. They made a glorious multi-coloured sight, swooping and shrieking through the air in victory rolls, singing a song of praise and thanks for the meal they had been given.

And then the barred gates opened again, the Song of the Sidewinders stopped abruptly and they instantly turned the colour of the sky again. Now it was they who were throwing themselves at the metal nets above them and finding they were trapped.

For creeping into the arena came twenty heavily armoured black Flashfangs, their razor-sharp teeth glistening in the sunshine, their talons making slashing patterns in the dust. The audience laughed cruelly at the fear of the Sidewinders, who seconds ago were the hunters and had now become the prey.

From his barred window high up in the Tower, Hiccup could watch no longer. He knew that a Sidewinder was no match for a Flashfang. He stepped away from the window with a heavy sigh.

Toothless had taken one look at the Flashfangs

and was now hiding in Hiccup's shirt.

The door of their prison cell opened with a crash. The First Kidnapper stepped in, followed by twenty heavily armed soldiers.

'Is the timings for your big day in the Circus,' beamed the First Kidnapper.

'Here goes...' said Camicazi grimly. 'Let us face certain death like HEROES.'

'It isn't *certain death*,' protested Hiccup. 'Don't forget my plan...'

'Would that be the plan where we get rescued at the last minute by a dragon the size of an amoeba?' asked Fishlegs.

The soldiers led the boys down from the Tower, across several courtyards and then down many long flights of steps so slippery Hiccup fell and grazed his calf. The steps ended in an underground chamber, where a Viking boat was tethered on the ground. On one side of the boat was painted its name: *The Valhalla Express*.

The chamber was beginning to fill with water – a dam in one of the chamber walls was open, and seawater was flooding in.

'Please to jump in,' grinned the First Kidnapper.

Camicazi was astonished. 'Are they setting us free, do you think?' she asked Hiccup.

'No chance,' replied Hiccup grimly. 'Look, they've half opened the gates of the dam... They think the ground isn't suitable for fighting on, like I said last night, so they're flooding the stadium. I thought they might do this... We're going to be part of a Sea-Battle for the entertainment of those Romans.'

'What about the F-F-Flashfangs?' asked Toothless from somewhere inside Hiccup's shirt.

'The water will kill the Flashfangs,' said Hiccup. 'Flashfangs can't swim... So who will WE be fighting, then? I suppose they'll put in a boat full of Roman gladiators – I've heard about these Sea-Battles.'

The First Kidnapper laughed. 'Waitings and seeings,' he said. The three Vikings and Toothless were now all aboard, the underground chamber was half full with water and the boat was bobbing clear of the ground. The Kidnapper gave them a cheery wave goodbye and cut the rope that moored *The Valhalla Express* to the dock.

18. THE VALHALLA EXPRESS

The Valhalla Express shot off down the tunnel, carried by the strong current of water.

The tunnel ended in a gate that led into the stadium. The gate was open and *The Valhalla Express* sailed into the central arena, now filled with three metres of water. Massive cheers rocked the stadium.

'FRIENDS AND FELLOW ROMANS!' yelled Alvin the Treacherous from the Consul's Pavilion. 'I GIVE YOU THE VALHALLA EXPRESS, THE HEIRS OF THE LOCAL VIKING TRIBES, AND THEIR PATHETIC CHAMPION DRAGON, TOOTHLESS, WHO WILL FOREVER REGRET THE POO HE DID IN MY HELMET.'

Always delighted to be the centre of attention, Toothless crept out from Hiccup's shirt. He bowed from side to side and performed a couple of somersaults to huge cheering from the crowd. He had no idea they were laughing at how small he was, and he puffed out his little chest and threw out a few flames and his rooster cry of self-congratulation.

'Now why,' said Hiccup, frowning to himself as he trailed one hand in the water, '*why* is this water so warm? I suppose it's from the Consul's swimming pool…'

Camicazi drew her sword, Invincible, with a flourish. 'LAUGH at us, would you, you Latin cowards?' she cried. 'Come down *here* if you dare and we'll see who's laughing *then*, shall we, you dragon-eating, lily-livered BABIES...'

The crowd positively SCREAMED with laughter at this. 'Look!' they cried, slapping each other on the back and sending their dragons'-toes popcorn flying. 'It's a little GIRL Viking! The Vikings are so weak they have GIRLS for Heirs! This is too funny for words...'

Camicazi couldn't understand Latin but she could guess what they were saying. She turned as red as a lobster and yelled at the top of her voice 'I'LL *KILL* THE LOT OF YOU! I'LL UNZIP YOU FROM YOUR BREADBASKETS TO YOUR FOOD-GARGLERS! COME DOWN AND SEE HOW A *GIRL* FIGHTS IF YOU DARE!'

The crowd only laughed the louder.

'Let's get on with it, Alvin!' Hiccup called out. 'Bring out your gladiators and we'll do our best!'

'Yes, do get on with it, Prefect,' yawned the Fat Consul. 'I want to see the little Berserk go Berserk... and this famous warrior in action...'

'HICCUP HORRENDOUS HADDOCK THE THIRD!' shouted Alvin. 'PREPARE TO MEET YOUR DOOM! SOLDIERS, OPEN THE TUNNEL!'

With a creak the portcullis covering a tunnel to their left began to slide upward…

19.
AAAAAAARGH!

The tunnel was open, but there was no sign of any Roman ships packed with heavily armed gladiators.

'What's going on?' shrieked Fishlegs. 'Where are the gladiators?'

Hiccup was staring intently at the tunnel. There still seemed to be nothing going on down there. All that came out of it were four long, dark waves – no more threatening than ripples, really.

The ripples curled sinuously into the stadium. Slowly, languorously, they began to circle the ship.

That's strange, thought Hiccup, and just as he was staring closely at one of the dark ripples, something neat and sharp cut through the surface of the water…

It was a black fin, with serrated edges like a bread-knife.

'SHARKWORMS!!!' yelled Fishlegs. 'I *knew* it! I just knew it! I knew we were going to

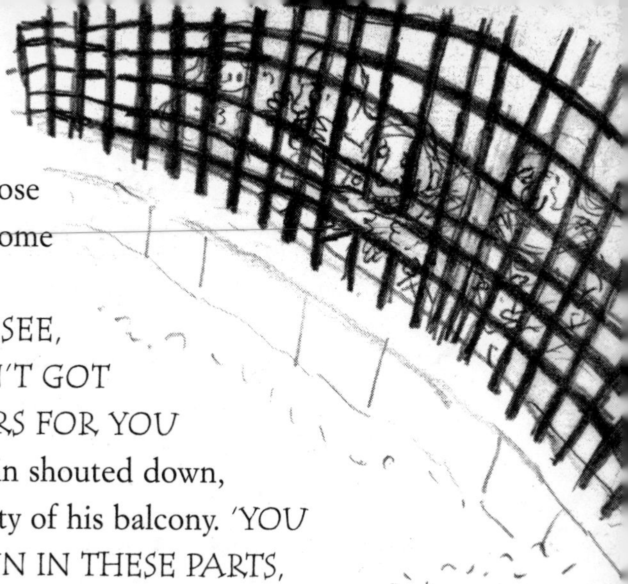

bump into those
monsters at some
point…'

'YOU SEE,
WE HAVEN'T GOT
GLADIATORS FOR YOU
TODAY,' Alvin shouted down,
from the safety of his balcony. 'YOU
ARE KNOWN IN THESE PARTS,
HICCUP, AS SOMETHING OF
A DRAGON-TRAINER – LET'S
SEE HOW YOU DO AT
TRAINING *THESE* LITTLE
BEAUTIES…'

'Is this part of your plan?' asked Camicazi
hopefully.

'Not exactly,'
admitted Hiccup. 'I
was expecting
gladiators – it *is* a

gladiator show, after all…'
'Can you TRAIN
them?' asked
Camicazi.
'What, in the next
sixty seconds?'
asked
Hiccup.

'Not
likely. Besides,
Sharkworms are
untrainable. The important
point is – has anybody got a
cut?'

'*You* have,' Fishlegs pointed
out. 'You fell over on the steps,
remember?'

'*Great*,' said Hiccup, glancing at the long
graze on his shin. 'Our lucky day. So, there's only
one thing to do. Nobody panic and I'll call for…
ZIGGERASTICA!'

Nothing happened.

The ripples had now turned into four Sharkworm fins, and they were circling nearer and nearer, closing in on the boat.

'ZIGGERASTICA!' screamed the Vikings all at once.

There was a streak of black and red and the tiny nanodragon appeared out of nowhere and landed on Camicazi's head.

'You called?' said Ziggerastica.

'About time too!' said Hiccup. 'How is the plan going?'

'It's a terrible plan,' said Ziggerastica, 'but so far the plan is going to plan, so to speak...'

'Everybody else, leave me!' urged Hiccup. 'Roll me into that barrel over there and throw me over the side!'

'What about the plan?' asked Fishlegs.

'This *is* the plan,' Hiccup replied.

'Oh I see,' said Fishlegs.

'When you said "desperate plan" you meant really *desperate*...'

'That *barrel* won't protect you from the Sharkworms!' protested Camicazi.

'Will you stop arguing and just do what I ask?' raged Hiccup. 'We're running out of time – those Sharkworms are going to climb on board any minute! It's me and my cut that they're really after...'

The Sharkworms were indeed circling the boat in tighter and tighter circles. Fishlegs could have reached out and touched one of the fins.

Fishlegs and Camicazi stuffed Hiccup into the barrel and Ziggerastica flew in with him. They then hesitated.

'Are you quite sure you want us to throw you over the side?' asked Fishlegs, looking in absolute terror at the fins slicing through the water.

'Quite sure,' came Hiccup's voice from the barrel, rather muffled.

'*With* the Sharkworms?' asked Camicazi.

'Just *do* it, will you!' yelled Hiccup.

Camicazi and Fishlegs reluctantly rolled the barrel over to the edge of the boat, heaved it up between them and dropped it over the side to the gasps of the watching audience.

'BRAVO!' the spectators cried, for the Romans admired bravery, even in a barbarian.

'It's such a shame,' whispered Camicazi. 'He was quite *nice* – for a *boy*, of course…'

The barrel bobbed merrily in the water.

Almost instantly the Sharkworms stopped following the boat and turned their attentions to the barrel. To start with they circled it in a leisurely way, almost as if they were sniffing it out. And then they began to move faster and faster around it, coming in closer and closer with more and more intent…

'Oh, H-H-HICCUP,' moaned Toothless, fluttering overhead with his wings over his eyes. 'I hope this is a really good plan…'

Inside the barrel Hiccup was hoping the very same thing. He was sitting up to his waist in water, unable to see out of the wooden walls of the barrel. The water was vibrating and the barrel was rocking from the wake of the Sharkworms' tails as they passed it.

He was regretting this stupid plan already. He couldn't see or hear anything but the horribly fast beating of his heart. And then the water in his barrel began to vibrate.

That's the sound of the Sharkworms calling to each other, thought Hiccup to himself, shivering uncontrollably.

CRASH!!

The barrel rocked crazily from side to side and Hiccup put both hands out to try to right it, frantically trying to see where the danger was coming from.

*That must be the wake from the Sharkworms'
tails as they pass*, he thought to himself, almost
hysterical with fear.

CRASH!!!

The barrel spun around again, more violently this
time. Hiccup was sent somersaulting upside down and
rolling over and over.

Watching from above, their hands over their
mouths, Camicazi and Fishlegs could see the
Sharkworms playing with the barrel almost as if they
were gigantic cats playing with a mouse. Toothless was
dive-bombing them, trying to attract their attention,
but they took no notice.

They batted the barrel to each other with the
wakes from their tails, but they hadn't touched it yet.

Suddenly they withdrew and reformed in a
slightly wider circle.

Inside the barrel Hiccup rose spluttering to the
surface. The barrel stopped spinning and there was
quiet again, apart from the lapping of the water against
the sides. Hiccup knew his dragons, he knew that they
would only have retreated to strike now in earnest.

He had to fight the urge to burst out of the barrel and swim for the boat.

He knew if he did this he was as good as dead.

But it was so scary not to be able to see what was going on, and so hard to stay completely still when he knew the beasts were all around him, could be underneath him, could be just a metre away, could strike suddenly at any moment from any direction…

C-C-CRUNCH!!!!!

The left-hand side of the barrel caved in as some immense force crashed into it. The wood just about held from splitting in half. Hiccup caught a glimpse of terrible black teeth no distance away from his nose before they retreated.

'Ziggerastica!' screamed Hiccup. 'HURRY UP!'

The Sharkworms were so close they were nearly touching each other now as they swam round and round. One of them let out a jet of fire like an underwater torpedo and the barrel burst into flames.

'And now, my clever friend,' said Alvin, watching the floating, flaming barrel with the four

predators surrounding it, 'O Defeater of the Seadragonus Giganticus Maximus and the Mighty Monstrous Strangulator – let's see you get out of THIS situation! I think I may safely say I've got you now...'

SPLASSSSSSSH!!!!

All four Sharkworms reared out of the water at the same time and spread out their wings.

They were a terrifying sight.

These two-headed beasts had eyes out on stalks, rather like a hammerhead shark. They were sometimes known as Thor's Lapdogs because of those hammer-shaped heads. Their back set of teeth could shoot forward to grab prey and then retreat back, dragging the unfortunate victim with them, as the tongue of a lizard flicks out to catch a fly.

Their hammerhead eyes swivelled on their stalks, their powerful tails lashed the water. They drew back their first sets of teeth in vicious snarls and the second sets shunted forward as if they had a life of their own, madly snapping together like an automatic killing mechanism.

For a moment they hovered in a terrible ring, their hammerhead eyes swivelling on their stalks to focus in on their target.

And then they let out a scream and pounced, all of them diving in on the barrel together...

CRACK!

The barrel split from side to side, and to the utter amazement of the watching Vikings, the audience, and the Sharkworms themselves... Hiccup FLEW out of it.

20. HICCUP THE GOD

The Romans flocked to the Circuses in their thousands to be entertained.

They expected a glorious theatrical experience – blood, guts, heroism, feats of astonishing physical prowess.

They were certainly getting their money's worth NOW.

This was a sight no one had ever seen before.

A flying boy?

The crowd leaped to their feet, amazed.

Fishlegs nearly fell out of the boat.

And slowly, majestically, Hiccup rose up through the rain with his arms spread out wide, as if held up by magical forces.

'Brilliant,' whispered Camicazi. 'I don't know HOW he's doing it, but it's brilliant.'

Hiccup rose and rose up to the metal 'ceiling' of the amphitheatre, the netting that the sharp teeth of the Flashfangs had failed to bite through in their terror…

At a single stroke of

Hiccup's
hand the netting
split in two...

He burst through
and hung in the air, every
awestruck eye upon him.

The Fat Consul fell to his knees. Even Alvin's
jaw dropped.

'MY NAME,' boomed Hiccup, in a voice he
had never used before, 'MY NAME IS THOR THE
THUNDERER, ANCIENT GOD OF THE VIKING
TRIBES!'

The crowd gasped.

'WELL MAY YOU TREMBLE,' bellowed
Hiccup. 'FOR YOU ROMANS HAVE INVADED
SACRED VIKING TERRITORIES AND MADE ME
MAD...'

'We're very, very sorry...' stammered the Fat
Consul.

'FOR THIS,' boomed Hiccup solemnly, 'I HAVE
SENT A PLAGUE UPON YOU AS THEIR
LEADER...'

The Consul scratched himself miserably.

'AND I SHALL PLAGUE YOU FOR EVER UNLESS YOU PROMISE TO GO FROM HERE AND NEVER RETURN.'

'We promise,' said the Consul. 'Here,' he sobbed, 'I offer you my shield, O Mighty One, as a sign of your protection from the Romans. Never again shall we come this far north.'

'I WILL TAKE YOUR SHIELD AS A SIGN OF YOUR PROMISE,' cried Hiccup, 'AND ALSO THE BOOK YOUR SERVANT STOLE FROM ME... OH, AND ONE MORE THING...'

'Anything, anything,' pleaded the Consul.

'I EXPECT YOU TO BE A STRICT VEGETARIAN FOR THE REST OF YOUR LIFE.'

The godlike Hiccup flew towards the Consul's balcony.

Still on his knees, the Consul offered him the rectangular Roman shield. Alvin put his trembling hand into his breast pocket and found the tattered copy of *How to Speak Dragonese*, the two halves sewn together carefully with golden Roman thread.

He fumbled to get rid of the booby trap he had placed inside the book. For Alvin was a careful man. He had slipped something *very nasty indeed* between the pages, a nanodragon called the Venomous Vorpent, so that anybody who tried to steal the book would get a horrible shock. But one does not booby-trap a god, and Alvin was desperately trying to shake out the poisonous nanodragon, when he caught a close-up sight of the shirt Hiccup was wearing...

'Hang on a second...' said Alvin.

But it was too late.

Hiccup snatched the book from him (still with the Venomous Vorpent inside it, please note), and rose swiftly into the air.

He held the shield victoriously above his head and made his final speech.

'I HOLD THE SHIELD AS A SIGN OF YOUR PROMISE... BUT IF YOU EVER BREAK THAT PROMISE, YOU CAN TELL YOUR CAESAR THAT THE FORCE OF MY ANGER SHALL REACH INTO THE HEART OF THE EMPIRE AND ROME HERSELF WILL BE SWEPT AWAY BY THE DELUGE...'

Hiccup pointed his sword at the dam.

Right on cue a couple of cracks appeared.

And the dam split in half and numberless tons of seawater burst into the stadium.

21. YOU CAN'T KEEP A BOG-BURGLAR UNDER LOCK AND KEY

The spell that Hiccup had cast on the audience was instantly broken.

It was as if they had been sleeping, and had suddenly woken up to the reality that they were about to be swept away by the flood.

Furthermore, everyone had forgotten about the Sharkworms. The metal netting that should have protected the audience had been broken by Hiccup. The Sharkworms were back in the water again and they were already nearly able to reach the wooden seating.

The audience screamed in terror as one of the Sharkworms leaped upward and was almost among them… it lost its grip on the slippery edge and fell back into the water – but the water was rising so quickly it was clearly only a matter of time before it succeeded in getting up to their level.

Suddenly the afternoon's entertainment of 'SURVIVAL OF THE FITTEST' had taken an interesting twist. The audience who had laughed so heartily at the tables being turned on the greedy Flashfangs didn't seem so amused to find they themselves had become the prey...

They stormed towards the entrance, shoving each other out of the way and screaming for the doors to be opened.

The pressure of the water on the doors caused them to open anyway. They burst apart and the water poured out and down the hillside.

Fishlegs and Camicazi turned their attention to steering the boat.

The flying Hiccup descended and landed beside them on the deck.

Toothless appeared from nowhere and perched on his shoulder.

'I am lost for words,' said Camicazi. 'How did you do it?'

Hiccup pointed to his shirt. 'Look a little closer,' he said.

The Vikings craned forward. Hiccup's shirt seemed to have changed colour. Indeed, when they looked closer still, it seemed not to be a shirt at all. It was made up of millions and millions of tiny winged creatures, all practically invisible to the naked eye and all clinging to Hiccup's clothing underneath. *This* was what had caused Hiccup to fly.

The numberless armies of Ziggerastica.

The little nanodragon himself flew out from his position of command on Hiccup's chest to bow to the Vikings.

'This terrible, terrible plan,' announced Ziggerastica joyfully, 'has worked beautifully. I, Ziggerastica the Mighty, have made it do this! How wonderful I am! How Glorious is my Empire! How numerous and powerful are my peoples!'

'We were lucky, too,' grinned Hiccup.

'I am almost sorry to leave you, O-Boy-With-No-Muscles-At-All,' said Ziggerastica sorrowfully. 'But we are quits now, I have saved your life in exchange for you saving mine and you are still a stinking HUMAN after all...'

'Thanks,' said Hiccup.

'But this has been a great day for the little creatures of the world ...'

Ziggerastica gave a single command and the nanodragons instantly rose in a grey mass, like a small thundercloud, and disappeared into the sky.

As they rose, they sang a

song that the Romans would have been
wise to listen to… but they were too busy panicking.

A WARNING TO EMPERORS

Watch out
O Romans with your Empires and your Stinking Breath
Watch out for the smaller things of this world
For we are going to get you… one day
You live your lives up in the skies
Building your aqueducts and your coliseums
And you never think of US
Ticking away in the grasses
But we see you
And if you bend your ear you just might hear
The steady beat of countless feet that come to eat
The wall that curls a hundred miles across a continent.
That temple built with the tears of millions of slaves
And all your most mighty and splendid creations
Shall turn to dust in our mouths
So watch out
O Caesars with Fat Bottoms and Hard Hearts
Watch out

'Goodbye, O-Boy-With-Arms-Like-Pieces-of-String...' sang Ziggerastica, 'and may the winds that blow you be strong...'

And with that, he was gone.

'Why did you let him go?' shrieked Fishlegs. 'I hate to mention this but we're not free yet, we're still stuck in an arena surrounded by Sharkworms!'

'The Sharkworms seem more interested in the audience,' said Hiccup. 'That's why I got Ziggerastica's armies to eat through the metal netting and to spend all night chomping through the dam. It was all part of my plan, you see – now the dam has cracked, we can simply sail out...'

Hiccup gestured to the open doors of the auditorium. The water was pouring out of them in a great river.

'Brilliant,' said Camicazi. 'I've got to admit, that's brilliant...for a boy, of course.'

Hiccup was already at the tiller and he pointed the ship towards the open doors of the stadium.

The Valhalla Express nosed its way towards the entrance.

'We're going to make it!' yelled Fishlegs. 'We're nearly there!'

The Valhalla Express was halfway through the door...

… but Alvin had spotted them trying to escape and given the order to send the portcullis rattling down. It cut The *Valhalla Express* in two. Fishlegs and Camicazi and Hiccup were thrown into the water on the wrong side of the bars. The sea was breath-quenchingly cold.

'AAAARGH!' shrieked Fishlegs, almost rearing out of the water, he was so terrified of the Sharkworms.

'Climb the portcullis,' ordered Hiccup.

The three young Vikings swam to the portcullis and climbed it, Hiccup towing Fishlegs, and with Toothless flapping behind them. Two metres or so up, they clung, dripping and terrified, like four little spiders.

Through the slippery bars they had a tantalising view of the freedom of the open ocean, hopelessly out of reach. All around them were the shrieks of the crowd, and clouds and clouds of escaping dragons. (The nanodragons had eaten the locks of those giant cages too.)

The Romans were running to their ships and setting sail back to Rome as fast as they could.

The Sharkworms were taking over the island,

climbing over the battlements and destroying the soldiers' tents. One or two of them had already made their way to the Fat Consul's swimming pool and were wallowing in the water.

'So what do we do now, then?' shouted Camicazi, her teeth chattering.

'I give up!' Hiccup shouted back, a sudden gust of wind nearly blowing him off the portcullis. His fingers were so frozen he wasn't sure how much longer he could hold on.

'This isn't part of my plan. What more do you want of me? It's all up to you now. *You're* the Master Escaper, aren't you? You're Ze Great Camicazi, no prison can hold you…'

'Ze Great Camicazi will get us out of here,' shouted Camicazi, 'if you admit that girls are way, way better than boys and always have been…'

'Dream on, sunshine,' grinned Hiccup.

'OK!' shouted Camicazi. 'Ze Great CAMICAZI will get us out of here anyway… You can't keep a Bog-Burglar under lock and key. Are you *sure* you want to follow me?'

'Lead on!' said Hiccup, with a slightly mad laugh. 'We can't hang around here for ever.'

Camicazi craned her neck upwards. Some way above them, tethered to the top of the amphitheatre entrance, was one of those enormous Roman observation balloons.

'If we can't *sail* our way out of here,' she yelled, 'I vote we *fly*!' and she pointed to the balloon.

'Ohhhh brother...' moaned Fishlegs miserably as he climbed slowly after the others, 'if Woden had meant us to fly he'd have given us wings... don't look down, Fishlegs – don't look down.'

Camicazi climbed expertly upwards, and she got to the balloon first, closely followed by Hiccup. They scrambled into the basket.

It was empty except for a rather depressed-looking Gronckle, trapped in a cage right underneath the open mouth of the balloon. Every now and then he shot out a burst of flame that heated the air, and this would send the balloon bouncing upward for a moment before it was stopped by the rope that moored it.

'Hello, Brother-of-the-Snake,' panted Hiccup. He looked carefully around the basket for any hidden soldiers. 'Are you on your own here?'

'The soldiers are all watching the Saturn's day

Saturday celebrations,' said the Gronckle. 'Actually, it's nice to have some peace and quiet for a change.'

'Well, I'm so sorry to disturb you,' said Hiccup, 'but we're taking over this balloon – it's a military emergency...'

'No problem,' said the sad Gronckle. 'It would be my pleasure. Nobody's bothered to ask me nicely before – they usually just hit me.'

'Oh dear,' said Hiccup sympathetically. He hated to see his fellow creatures trapped or ill-treated. 'Of course we'll let you go as soon as we get home, but at the moment we're in a bit of a hurry.'

'It's not that I don't like the job,' the Gronckle assured him. 'It's nice up here – peaceful, you know. When would you like to leave?'

'Very soon,' said Hiccup. 'We're just waiting for a friend.' He peered back over the edge of the basket. He could see the top of Fishlegs's head, making painfully slow progress up the portcullis. Below him, the excitable Sharkworms leaped, and the crowds stampeded. 'FISHLEGS! Will you get a move on!'

'I'm climbing as fast as I can!' Fishlegs shouted back up indignantly. 'I'm not stopping to admire the view or anything!'

'H-h-he'd better make it quick,' advised Toothless into Hiccup's ear. 'Toothless s-s-sees that nasty Alvin coming our way.'

Sure enough, Alvin was running towards them along the top of the battlements.

'You try and DELAY him, Toothless,' Hiccup ordered. 'FISHLEEEGS! YOU REALLY, REALLY NEED TO HURRY UP!'

Toothless held Alvin up by attacking his toga. 'I should have killed you while I had the chance, you wretched reptile,' cursed Alvin, lashing out with his hook and trying to catch him, while Fishlegs climbed the last couple of metres.

Hiccup helped haul Fishlegs into the basket and Camicazi cut the rope. 'GO, GO, GO!' yelled Camicazi and the Gronckle sent a bright breath of flame up into the balloon and it rose off the battlements into the air.

But just as it rose, a golden hook clunked into the bottom of the basket and held fast.

The Gronckle gave another big puff and the great balloon shot gracefully upwards, and the grim hook, together with Alvin the Treacherous, shot up too.

'S-s-sorry,' said Toothless, crash-landing on

Hiccup's helmet. 'I couldn't keep him back any longer.'

Fishlegs glanced over the basket's side then looked at Hiccup with popping eyes. 'Oohh, dear, is that who I think it is?' he moaned. 'It's like a nightmare – we can't get rid of him!'

Hiccup dared himself to take a look over the rim.

There was Fort Sinister, rapidly getting smaller as they rose away from it.

And there, swinging from the bottom of the basket by his hook alone, was Alvin the Treacherous.

He made a savage swipe at Hiccup with his free arm and Hiccup ducked quickly back into the safety of the basket.

'Right,' said Hiccup. 'I wouldn't put it past him to climb in from that position... Everybody start running clockwise. Toothless, I want you to grab this rope and pull it in the same direction. We have to get this balloon spinning around...'

All together, they began to run and the balloon began to spin, slowly at first and then with gathering speed, round and round and round like *The Hopeful Puffin* having one of her turns.

And as that balloon spun it slowly, slowly, slowly unscrewed the hook of Alvin the Treacherous.

He felt his hook loosening and realised what was happening but there was nothing he could do. 'I'll get you, Hiccup Horrendous Haddock the Third!' cursed Alvin as the hook unscrewed as far as it would go, 'I'll get you one daaaaaaaay!' and he plunged downwards into the sea and a mass of waiting Sharkworms, leaving only a great, golden hook swinging from the bottom of the basket.

The balloon soared upwards, and as the screams of Alvin grew fainter and fainter so too did the shrieks

of the dragons, and the whole wild cacophony of Fort Sinister died away in a matter of moments.

Hiccup, Fishlegs and Camicazi slumped to the floor of the basket.

Quietly, softly, the balloon drifted on. The only sound was the gentle puffs of the Gronckle's flames, and the panting of the Vikings as they caught their breaths, their hearts beginning to slow down. Gradually, they smiled at one another as they realised that they might, just possibly, be safe at last.

'Phew,' said Camicazi, bright red in the face, 'that was a close one… What did I tell you? You can't keep a Bog-Burglar under lock and key. And you didn't do too badly… for boys, of course.'

Hiccup staggered to his feet and peered over the edge of the basket.

A warm breeze blew his hair back.

'Look!' cried Hiccup, pointing downwards and then turning back to the others in sudden excitement. 'My father's War Party! He did send it after all!'

'Well, I don't know what you're so pleased about – it's a bit *late*, don't you think?' grumbled Fishlegs. 'One day earlier and it could have saved me about three thousand heart attacks…'

'It doesn't matter,' grinned Hiccup. 'He *sent* it, and that's the important thing. He doesn't think Snotlout would make a better Heir after all.'

22. THE RETURN OF THE HEROIC HEIRS

On the deck of *The Blue Whale*, Stoick the Vast waited to receive a visit from Chief Big-Boobied Bertha Bog-Burglar, who was about to come aboard.

Stoick had decided on Plan B, send out the Rescue War Party, rather than Plan A, fight the Bog-Burglars, but Big-Boobied Bertha was making Plan B difficult to carry out by following the Hooligan Rescue War Party with the entire Bog-Burglar Navy the whole way from Berk.

So Stoick had sent a Carrier Dragon with a (very polite) message to Big-Boobied Bertha suggesting that they talk things through. And now he was pacing up and down, trying to tell himself how Hiccup would act in this situation. 'I have to stay calm,' he muttered. 'Hiccup was right – these blood feuds will be the death of us Vikings and it is my job as Chief to put a stop to them…'

'I hope you're going to bash this Big-boobied Bertha Bog-Burglar Chieftain on the nose, Stoick!' roared Baggybum the Beerbelly. 'If *you* don't do it, I might have to myself…'

'The only good Bog-Burglar is a dead Bog-Burglar,' sneered Snotlout. Snotlout was feeling extremely pleased with the way things were turning out. It looked like Hiccup was finally out of his way, and now they could have a big fight with the Bog-Burglars and Snotlout could show off about what a great fighter he was…

Stoick ignored both of them and went on with his pacing. 'I have to explain to Big-Boobied Bertha – *calmly* – that I think the Romans have stolen our Heirs and that is why I am sending out this War Party. I have to stay calm at all times…'

Big-Boobied Bertha stomped on board, her beard bristling. Fists like sledgehammers, ears like cauliflowers, she had once stunned a stag with one blow of her mighty bosoms, and many a smaller animal had suffocated in their stern depths. She gave Baggybum the Beerbelly an arrogant shove out of the way, and stood in front of Stoick with her hands on her hips.

Stoick swallowed hard. He could feel his ears beginning to burn. 'Stay calm, Stoick,' he warned himself. 'Ohhh, this is going to be hard…'

BIG-BOOBIED BERTHA

These bosoms have killed before and they will kill again...

It was going to be impossible.

'I ALWAYS KNEW YOU WERE A FAT BURGLAR AND AN HEIR-STEALER,' roared Big-Boobied Bertha, 'BUT I NEVER KNEW YOU WOULD RUN AWAY LIKE A COWARDLY JELLYFISH!'

'I WAS NOT RUNNING AWAY!' yelled Stoick. He nearly exploded with the effort of trying to control himself. 'Now, calm at all times, Stoick – calm at all times, remember,' he muttered, before continuing. 'I have strong reasons to believe that our Heirs have been stolen by the Romans. I am sending out this Rescue War Party—'

'STRONG REASONS MY BOTTOM!' boomed Big-Boobied Bertha. 'YOU WERE RUNNING AWAY BECAUSE HOOLIGANS ARE THE YELLOWEST BABY RABBITS IN THE INNER ISLES!'

'THIS HOOLIGAN COULD TAKE YOU WITH ONE HAND BEHIND HIS BACK AND ONLY USING HIS LITTLE FINGER!' screamed Stoick the Vast, and there was a strong chance that Plan B might have turned rapidly back into Plan A again if the two Chiefs – who were nose to nose, yelling at one another – had not heard a noise that made them look suddenly upwards, where they saw, to their astonishment, an enormous Roman observation balloon descending very rapidly in their direction. The Bog-Burglars and the Hooligans had been so busy focusing on each other that they hadn't even noticed the balloon above them. But they certainly noticed it now, as it was partly deflated and screaming towards the deck of *The Blue Whale* at about a hundred miles an hour.

*   *   *

When they spotted the Hooligan War Party, it was Hiccup who suggested that they try and land the balloon on one of the ships. He got the sad Gronckle to stop blowing flames so the balloon could descend, and he got Toothless to take a rope in his mouth to steer the balloon in the right direction.

'Work, w-w-work, work,' grumbled Toothless. 'Why can't somebody else do it?'

'Because you're the only one with wings, Toothless,' explained Hiccup patiently.

Camicazi half hung over the edge of the balloon

as it descended, enjoying the wind blowing through her hair. 'You've got to hand it to those Romans they are CLEVER! This is the only way to travel… I wonder if WE could build one of these things? Hey – aren't they my MOTHER'S boats alongside the Hooligan ships?'

Hiccup leaned over to check. 'So they are,' he said in surprise. 'Maybe the grown-ups saw sense at last and decided to send a joint Rescue Party! I must say I'm amazed – that's a real sign of progress for the Viking Tribes.'

The descent would have continued in this controlled fashion if it hadn't been for the little booby trap that Alvin the Treacherous had slipped between the pages of *How to Speak Dragonese* when he returned it to Hiccup.

The booby trap was a tiny little bright yellow dragon, about the size of Ziggerastica, known as the Venomous Vorpent.

This particular Vorpent had crawled out of Hiccup's pocket, had a long slow look around the basket while everyone was relaxing, and then begun to climb up Fishlegs's trouser leg.

Fishlegs only noticed it when it began to walk

The
VENOMOUS
VORPENT

This bright yellow nanodragon carries poison in both the glands, in its neck and also its tail. The sting of a Venomous Vorpent is absolutely always fatal.

~STATISTICS~

COLOURS: Bright Yellow.

ARMED WITH: Deadly Venom...... 15

POISON: (see above).... 15

SIZE: Teeny Weeny

FEAR AND FIGHT FACTOR: Do NOT Tread on this animal... 15

Close relative THE SAND RATTLER

across his hand, and then he let out a scream and flicked his hand so that the Vorpent sailed upwards and the immensely pointy sting in his tail tore a great rip in the surface of the balloon.

The descent then became a bit more rapid.

Stoick the Vast and Big-Boobied Bertha jumped apart and the basket of the balloon crashed on to the deck between them.

The balloon itself became entangled in the sails of *The Blue Whale*.

There was an astonished silence, and then one by one, the sad Gronckle, Toothless, Camicazi, Fishlegs and Hiccup came crawling out of the tipped-over basket.

*　　*　　*

Great were the celebrations in the Hooligan and Bog-Burglar Tribes when they realised their Heirs had been returned to them unharmed. The battle songs being beaten out on the War Drums turned to songs of triumph. The two great snaky lines of warships rang out with cheers and the Warriors fired their arrows into the air in their joy. (Which incidentally is not to be recommended – someone could take their eye out doing that. But Hooligans and Bog-Burglars were not known for their common sense.)

Stoick hugged his son and said no words… but Hiccup knew what he meant.

'Stoick,' Big-Boobied Bertha said at last, as she lifted her daughter on to her mighty shoulders in triumph, 'by way of apology, I would like to give you a little gift.'

Big-Boobied Bertha clapped her hands and one of her Warriors brought forward a gigantic shield.

'Waistline of Woden!' exclaimed Fishlegs, staring down at the shield. 'You realise what this *is*, don't you? It's only the shield of Grimbeard the Ghastly!'

It was indeed Grimbeard the Ghastly's famous shield, taken in battle by the Bog-Burglars many years before and held by the Tribe as a trophy ever since.

Perfectly round, in the centre was a skull crowned by seaweed, around which waves and dragons chased each other in an endless circle.

Snotlout's eyes gleamed.

Snotlout was feeling extremely put out. Here was Hiccup turning up, YET AGAIN not dead, not drowned and not eaten by Sharkworms, and it didn't look like there was going to be a fight after all.

But now he saw he could prove *he* was destined to be Chief not Hiccup.

Snotlout picked up the shield of Grimbeard the Ghastly and held it victoriously over his head.

It was a glorious moment. Snotlout looked magnificent, standing there nobly, all muscly and tattooed, with the last rays of the setting sun blazing over the horizon and sending flashes of silver off the shield and into the sky.

The watching Hooligans, some of whom were not very sure what was going on and all of whom were not very bright, assumed that Snotlout had saved the day in some way. He certainly looked good. They started shouting 'SNOT-LOUT! SNOT-LOUT! SNOT-LOUT!' and the Bog-Burglars replied with cries of 'CAMI-CAZI! CAMI-CAZI! CAMI-CAZI!'

'Oh for Thor's sake!' said Fishlegs. 'I'm not having *this* happening all over again! This was nothing to do with you, Snotlout – you weren't even THERE, for Thor's sake! It was *Hiccup* who just saved all our lives, *Hiccup* who had the clever plan, and *Hiccup* is the Heir to the Hairy Hooligans!'

'PUSH him, Fishlegs,' advised Camicazi from her mother's shoulder.

Fishlegs gave Snotlout a big shove in the stomach.

Ordinarily, Fishlegs would never have been able to push Snotlout over. But the shield Snotlout was holding above his head made him a little unsteady. He fell overboard into the water with an enormous splash.

There was a bit of a horrified silence.

And then Chief Stoick the Vast threw back his great hairy head and shouted out 'HA HA HA!' in a huge guffaw.

The cheers of the watching Tribes turned to great yells of laughter, for there is nothing they enjoy more than a really simple joke where someone falls over or gets wet or covered in mud. So they laughed as long and loudly and rudely as only Vikings can – splitting their sides and bending over double and thumping each other on their hairy backs – as the sun set on Saturn's day Saturday in a spectacular display of red and pink and gold.

Snotlout was pulled out of the sea by his father, Baggybum the Beerbelly, still clinging on to the shield of Grimbeard the Ghastly. And even Snotlout was forced to join in the laughter so he didn't look like a bad sport.

'Hiccup,' said Stoick at last, wiping the tears from his eyes. '*I have a present for you…*'

Stoick led Hiccup over to the back of *The Blue Whale* and there, being dragged behind by a rope, was the familiar sight of a small, fat boat with a slightly wonky mast and a drunken wobble to the left…

'*The Hopeful Puffin!*' exclaimed Hiccup joyfully.

'Gobber dived down into the Harbour and brought her up for you,' beamed Stoick.

'I mended a couple of holes for you,' boomed Gobber, slapping Hiccup on the back. 'We'll make a Viking of you yet.'

'Maybe you and your dragon, Juiceless, and Fisheggs and Cami-whatsit here could lead us back to Berk in triumphal procession?' said Stoick. 'After all, it's not *every* day that the noble Tribes of Bog-Burglar and Hooligan have their Heirs returned to them…'

As darkness fell all around them, the islands of the Archipelago turned from green to grey and then to black, and the Viking Warriors lit the flares that hung along the sides of the gently rocking ships.

The Electricsquirms flickered into life and danced across the ocean like little fiery sparks, trailing tails of sparkling, dusty light behind them.

The sea was as flat as glass, and the reflection of the full moon in the water made a flickering path of moonbeams, leading all the way up to the distant silhouette of the Isle of Berk on the horizon.

Hiccup and Toothless and Fishlegs and Camicazi climbed on board *The Hopeful Puffin*, who seemed none the worse for having been down to the bottom of the ocean and come back up again.

And if a stranger could have observed that night-time procession they would have thought it odd indeed to see the progress of the Viking warships that night.

For were not the Vikings supposed to be the Masters of the Seas, the greatest pirates and navigators the world has ever known?

And now here were these two great, snaking,

flaming lines of Hooligan and Bog-Burglar ships, zigzagging wildly this way and that, turning round in circles and doubling back on themselves, laughing and apologising and cursing in the darkness.

They were all following the lead of one tiny boat at the front, *The Hopeful Puffin*, as she twirled and span and revolved in her own peculiar way across the path of the moon towards Berk.

EPILOGUE BY HICCUP HORRENDOUS HADDOCK THE THIRD, THE LAST OF THE GREAT VIKING HEROES

Here I am, back where I started; this all happened such a long, long time ago.

But now I come to think of it, if I look around the desk where I am writing now I can see things all around me that remind me of that time.

The hook of Alvin the Treacherous hangs on my wall like a golden question mark. By the door rests the shield given to me by the Fat Consul.

I have taken that shield into battle with me all my life, much to the amusement of my friends, for instead of being circular like Viking shields it is square in the Roman fashion.

But then I have always been somewhat of a square peg in a round hole.

Even the quill with which I am writing now is made out of a Roman golden eagle's feather that I found in my cell at Fort Sinister.

I look at these things and I remember, and what I remember most clearly is the moment when the balloon rose out of the jabber and hullabaloo of the prison of Fort Sinister and into the clear blue sky like a perfectly round bubble of happiness, or a balloon of thought.

I remember the quiet stillness of that moment, floating free of all care and worry, suspended magically in the endless nothingness of the air below and above us.

I remember my child-self looking down over the rim of the basket and seeing my entire world laid out beneath me like a map in a made-up story. For the first time I saw that the place where I lived and struggled and worried was part of an Archipelago of staggering beauty: hundreds of tiny green islands set in a shimmering blue sea.

And suddenly I realised with such clearness what pinpricks we were on this ocean universe. What swaggering insects! What posturing amoebas!

But size isn't everything, as I am always telling Snotlout. However small we are, we should always fight for what we believe to be right. And I don't mean fight with the power of our fists or the power of our swords. That has always been the problem with us Vikings. I mean the power of our brains and our thoughts and our dreams.

And as small and quiet and unimportant as our fighting may look, perhaps we might all work together like the numberless armies of Ziggerastica, and break out of the prisons of our own making. Perhaps we might be able to keep this fierce and beautiful world of ours as free *for all of us* as it seemed to be on that blue afternoon of my childhood.

Once, my hand held the sword 'Endeavour' so strongly. Now that same hand is as brown and wrinkly as an old salt kipper as it writes these words slowly and shakily across the page. The ink splutters and splodges where once it ran so smoothly. Sometimes I forget what I was doing last Tuesday, let alone sixty-five years ago.

But the winds will still blow when I am no longer here. The storms will still rage, and the forces of

Empire and oppression, be they Roman or otherwise, will still be waiting at the corners of the ocean.

The fight goes on for the Heroes of the Future.

The Sting in the Tale

Surely, surely, that must be the end of **Alvin the Treacherous,** *last seen dropping from a height into a heaving mass of Sharkworms? And surely, surely there must be a happy ending at last for all our Viking warriors large and small?*

But as with many happy endings, there is a sting in the tale. In this case, unknown to everybody, in the confusion when the balloon fell out of the sky, one of our Heroes was stung with a single drop of poison from the terrible tail of the Venomous Vorpent.

And, as everybody knows, the sting of the Venomous Vorpent is absolutely always fatal…

Which of our Heroes was unlucky enough to be stung?

Look out for the next volume of Hiccup's memoirs…

I don't like happy endings.

They are too neat, too nice.

I like a little spice in my stories.

So this is NOT a happy ending.

It is just 'Toodleooonseeyasoon...',

Which is Dragonese for 'the story continues'.

Read more of Hiccup's memoirs…

HOW TO TRAIN YOUR DRAGON
by Hiccup Horrendous Haddock III
Translated from the Old Norse
by Cressida Cowell

Hiccup Horrendous Haddock III was a truly extraordinary Viking hero, known throughout the Viking kingdom as 'the dragon whisperer' on account of his power over these terrifying beasts. But it wasn't always like that …

In fact, in the beginning, Hiccup was the most put-upon Viking you'd ever seen. Not loud enough to make himself heard at dinner with his father, Stoick the Vast; not hard enough to beat his chief rival, Snotlout, at Bashyball, and CERTAINLY not able to control his lazy dragon Toothless!

Read about Hiccup Horrendous Haddock III's rise to fame and desperate dragon-training exploits.